Also by R. A. Spratt

The Adventures of Nanny Piggins
Nanny Piggins and the Wicked Plan
Nanny Piggins and the Runaway Lion
Nanny Piggins and the Accidental Blast-Off
Nanny Piggins and the Rival Ringmaster
Nanny Piggins and the Pursuit of Justice
Nanny Piggins and the Daring Rescue
Nanny Piggins and the Race to Power
The Nanny Piggins Guide to Conquering Christmas

Friday Barnes: Girl Detective
Friday Barnes: Under Suspicion
Friday Barnes: Big Trouble

R. A. Spratt

FRIDAY BARNES

No Rules

RANDOM HOUSE AUSTRALIA

A Random House book
Published by Random House Australia Pty Ltd
Level 3, 100 Pacific Highway, North Sydney NSW 2060
www.randomhouse.com.au

Penguin
Random House
Australia

First published by Random House Australia in 2016

Random House Books is part of the Penguin Random House group of companies whose addresses can be found at global.penguinrandomhouse.com.

National Library of Australia
Cataloguing-in-Publication Entry

Author: Spratt, R. A.
Title: No Rules
ISBN: 978 0 85798 701 3 (pbk)
Series: Friday Barnes; 4
Subject: Girls – Juvenile fiction
        Detective and mystery stories
Dewey Number: A823.4

Cover illustration by Lilly Piri
Cover design by Kirby Armstrong
Internal design and typesetting by Midland Typesetters, Australia
Printed in Australia by Griffin Press, an accredited ISO AS/NZS 14001:2004 Environmental Management System printer

Random House Australia uses papers that are natural, renewable and recyclable products and made from wood grown in sustainable forests. The logging and manufacturing processes are expected to conform to the environmental regulations of the country of origin.

To Violet and Samantha

Chapter 1

Where We Left Off

Friday was in a good mood as she entered the dining hall at Highcrest Academy with the Headmaster, her best friend Melanie Pelly, and Ian Wainscott, the most handsome boy in school. The Headmaster had promised Friday an extra serving of dessert for helping Highcrest avert their latest near disaster. An impostor had impersonated a member of the Norwegian royal family and gone on a school-wide theft spree.

But Friday and her friends never got to eat that ice-cream.

As they walked in, Friday's Uncle Bernie was there waiting for her, and with him were a man and a woman wearing dark grey suits and sunglasses.

'Who are they?' asked the Headmaster.

'The big scruffy man in the creased suit is my Uncle Bernie,' said Friday.

'Perhaps soon to be Ian's stepdad,' added Melanie.

'He is not!' said Ian.

'And the other two,' said Friday, 'given their suits with a high polyester count and ostentatious wearing of sunglasses, I deduce are some sort of government officials.'

'Friday!' exclaimed Uncle Bernie as soon as he saw her. 'I'm so sorry. There's nothing I can do.'

'About what?' she asked.

The woman pulled an identification card from her pocket. 'I'm Agent Torres from the Department of Immigration. Are you Friday Barnes?'

'Yes, that's me,' said Friday.

'Then you'll have to come with us,' said Agent Torres.

'Why?' asked Friday.

'You're being deported,' said Uncle Bernie.

'Hang on, I'm headmaster here, I'm responsible for this child,' said the Headmaster.

'All the paperwork is in order,' said Agent Torres. The other agent handed a sheaf of paperwork to the Headmaster. He started flicking through it.

'On what grounds can you deport her?' asked the Headmaster. 'She hasn't committed a crime. Well . . . not one that's been proven, anyway.'

'We're deporting her because she's not a citizen,' said Agent Torres.

'Yes, I am,' said Friday.

'Is it true you were born in Switzerland?' asked Agent Torres.

'Well, yes,' conceded Friday.

'And you have never applied for citizenship or even a permanent residency visa?' said the agent.

'I was a baby,' said Friday. 'I assumed that was all sorted out when my parents brought me home . . . Oh no, my parents! They never filled in the paperwork, did they?'

'No, they didn't,' said Uncle Bernie. 'If I'd known about it sooner, I could have done something.'

'The Department of Immigration has been writing to them, phoning them and even visiting them

3

repeatedly over the years,' said Agent Torres. 'They have ignored all our correspondence. Dr Evangeline Barnes and Dr Rupert Barnes are no longer residents of the country. You are a Swiss citizen who has been illegally residing in this country for twelve years. You will be deported today.'

'But . . .' protested Friday.

'If you want to appeal the decision,' said Agent Torres, 'you'll have to take it up with our embassy in Geneva.'

'But wait until Wednesday,' advised Melanie. 'We've got PE on Tuesday and we're playing dodgeball. You'll want to miss that.'

The agents grabbed Friday by an elbow each and started leading her away. Friday got one last glance at her friends before she was ushered out the door.

Melanie turned to the Headmaster. 'She will be back, won't she?'

'I hope so,' said the Headmaster, rubbing his head in anticipation of the headache he knew he was about to get. 'It's hard enough running this school. Who's going to figure out all the weird hijinks that go on if Friday isn't here?'

'I'm sure it will all be sorted out in just a couple of days,' said Uncle Bernie.

Chapter 2

▰▰▰▰▰▰▰▰▰▰▰▰▰▰

Lounging in Transit

Friday Barnes had been living in the transit lounge at Zurich international airport for three weeks. This was actually nowhere near as unpleasant as it sounds. Usually people loathe time in a transit lounge because they are anxiously awaiting a flight that has probably been delayed and they have an inherent phobia of flying.

But Friday had taken up residence. Technically, she wasn't a citizen of anywhere. The Swiss authorities

5

would not let her through border control, so she was stuck. Friday couldn't go home because she didn't have a passport or visa. And she couldn't leave the airport and go into Zurich because the Swiss government didn't acknowledge her citizenship.

Again, this sounds like a deeply unpleasant limbo to a normal person, but Friday was far from normal. She was having a very pleasant time. She was able to earn a nice living by acting as a translator for confused travellers. She got plenty to eat in the first class lounges run by the different airlines, because they would each exchange access to their lounge for her translating services, or get her to fix their computers. She even received letters care of Mr Tanaka at the airport's sushi bar, so Melanie was able to write to her.

Dear Friday,

I wish you would hurry up and get yourself re-imported home. School is not the same without you. In biology this morning Mr Poshoglian actually asked me a question. He would never do that if you were here. He is normally so busy avoiding eye contact with you that he never notices me.

Ian misses you. Of course, you can't tell from anything he says or does, but it's true. I think he's up to something. It's a shame you're not here to nip it in the bud before he gets himself into trouble.

I've got to go. I can barely keep my eyes open. I don't know how people in the olden days coped with letter-writing. Handwriting is exhausting.

Bye for now,
Melanie xxoo

And unlike Highcrest Academy, the transit lounge had free internet access, so Friday was able to keep in touch with her Uncle Bernie, who was doing all he could to get the embassy to take action. Friday was video-chatting with him.

'You'd think the child of a Nobel Laureate would have an easier time getting a passport,' grumbled Uncle Bernie. 'But the hard part was getting someone from the embassy to make the three-hour drive from Geneva to Zurich Airport to sort it all out.'

'Petrol is expensive,' said Friday reasonably.

'You're a twelve-year-old living in an airport,' said Uncle Bernie. 'Where's their compassion?'

'I'm having a perfectly nice time,' said Friday.

'Don't tell them that,' said Uncle Bernie. 'They'll never get you out.'

'I'm fine,' said Friday. 'You're much more upset than I am.'

'I just feel so guilty,' said Uncle Bernie. 'If I hadn't been rude to the receptionist at the embassy that first time I rang up, they wouldn't have put me on the no-fly list and I could have travelled to Switzerland to meet with the embassy officials myself.'

'It's all right,' said Friday. 'It's only been three weeks. I'm learning so much here in the airport. It's wonderful to have the opportunity to try out so many of the languages I've been studying.'

'Friday, you're not meant to be enjoying yourself,' said Uncle Bernie. 'If you were hysterical and weeping, it might help motivate some people.'

'Sorry, Uncle Bernie,' said Friday. 'Hysterical and weeping just isn't in my nature. I don't think I'm in touch enough with my emotions. I'd prefer to suppress everything, then let it all well out in six or seven years' time when I buy a puppy dog.'

'Friday Barnes, please report to immigration control. Friday Barnes,' said a voice over the airport PA system.

'I think I'm being paged,' said Friday.

'Entschuldigen, Friday, they're calling you!' called Alexander the barista from the coffee shop. 'I hope this is good for you, yes?'

'Me too,' said Friday. She spoke to the webcam. 'Sorry, Uncle Bernie, I've got to go. I'm being paged by immigration control. This could be it.'

'That's wonderful!' said Uncle Bernie. 'If they interview you, remember, whatever you do – don't be yourself. Try to act like a normal person.'

'I'm not going to make promises I can't keep,' said Friday. 'Bye, Uncle Bernie, I'll let you know how it goes.' She logged off and grabbed her duffle bag.

'Here, take a cookie for luck,' said Alexander.

'Thanks,' said Friday as she gathered up her things, grabbed the cookie and jogged towards the passport check lines.

'Friday,' called Gunter the immigration official. He waved happily from the kiosk near the security check. 'They've finally got a bigwig out to see you.' Gunter opened a gate so she could enter the office area.

'What sort of bigwig?' asked Friday.

'Some suited man from the embassy. Perhaps they're going to spring you from here,' said Gunter.

'I'll be happy for you, but I'll be sorry to see you go. Marika has been doing much better at school since you've been coaching her in maths.'

'Skill in mathematics is so good for a girl's self-esteem,' said Friday.

'Anyway, he's waiting in interview room one for you,' said Gunter. He led Friday through a private door into a corridor flanked by interview rooms.

'Herr Quigley, here she is,' said Gunter. 'You should snap her up for your country quickly. We might have a tough citizenship process here in Switzerland, but it's only a matter of time before someone realises what an asset she is to any nation.'

Friday stepped into the room. A serious-looking man in a grey suit was sitting at the interview table checking messages on his mobile phone as he made notes on a writing pad. Friday's files were sitting closed on the table. This was the man who could decide Friday's fate and everything about him said 'bureaucrat'. He was neat, bland and conservative.

'Yes, all right –' said Mr Quigley, then his phone started ringing. 'Excuse me, I have to take this.'

Friday looked at Gunter and raised her eyebrows.

'Good luck,' said Gunter. He patted her on the shoulder before he left.

'No, no. I'll be back there as soon as possible,' Mr Quigley was saying into the phone. 'Tell him I'll call him back . . . Okay, tell her I'll call her back . . . A four-foot-tall ice sculpture can't just go missing. It's got to be somewhere. Just tell them all I'll call them once I finish this meeting and I'm back in my car.'

'You shouldn't talk on the phone while you're driving,' interrupted Friday.

'Shhh,' said Mr Quigley, looking up at Friday for the first time. Then someone on the other end of the phone evidently yelled in his ear because he flinched. 'No, not *you*, there's a girl in the room talking to me.'

'When you talk on the phone while you're driving, you are 34 per cent more likely to have or cause a traffic accident,' said Friday.

'I have a hands-free set-up,' said Mr Quigley, holding his hand over the mouthpiece as he spoke to Friday.

'That's only marginally safer,' said Friday. 'True, you can use both hands to drive the car, but you are still distracted by the conversation, and unlike a conversation with a car passenger, the person on the other end of the phone doesn't instinctively stop talking when you reach a point of critical decision-making – such as when you're changing lanes in high-speed traffic or making your way through a busy junction.'

'I've got to hang up,' Mr Quigley said to the person on the phone. 'I think this meeting is going to be more difficult than I imagined.' He put his phone down on the table. 'Now, Miss . . .' Mr Quigley checked his file. 'Scheunen, Freitag Scheunen.'

'My name is Friday Barnes,' said Friday.

'Yes, well, technically that is your alias,' said Mr Quigley, double-checking the details in his paper-work. 'Since you have no passport, your only official record is your birth certificate and it's got you down as Freitag Scheunen.'

'That's German for Friday Barns,' said Friday. 'Freitag means "Friday" and Scheunen means "barns", as in the large farm buildings. But I'm Barnes with an "e".'

'The German version is your official name,' said Mr Quigley.

'I'll be sure to change it officially as soon as I get home,' said Friday.

Mr Quigley's phone started ringing again.

'Excuse me,' said Mr Quigley as he picked it up. 'Hello. Ahuh . . . No, I'll speak to him myself when I get back. I don't know! It will go quicker if people stop calling me all the time! Okay . . . okay . . . I hear what you're saying. I'm sorry I raised my voice. No, there's no need to file a complaint with human resources. I promise it won't happen again.' Mr Quigley put his phone on the table.

'Why don't you turn it off?' asked Friday. 'We'll deal with my problem quicker than you'll be able to get back to your crisis at the embassy.'

'I can't turn my phone off,' said Mr Quigley.

'Why not?' asked Friday.

'It would be irresponsible. I'm secretary to the Ambassador. I have to be on call 24/7.'

The phone started ringing again. Friday snatched it up, turned it off and laid it face-down on the table.

'Hey!' exclaimed Mr Quigley. 'That's government property. If you're applying for citizenship, this isn't helping you.'

'No, perhaps not,' said Friday. 'But how about I help you? I think it will be the quickest way to get you to focus on my problems.'

'What?' said Mr Quigley.

'If you've read my file,' said Friday, 'which I doubt you have because you are clearly of the belief that you are too important for such a menial task. But if you had read it, you would know that I have been very successful as a private detective.'

'You're twelve years old,' said Mr Quigley. 'I read that much of your file.'

'Yes, which is what makes my success at solving crime so impressive,' said Friday. 'Tell me about your problem. I bet I can help.'

'I can't tell you about embassy business,' said Mr Quigley. 'It's confidential.'

'You see, this is an example of why you're deluded about your own self-importance,' said Friday. 'I actually know what your problem is because I've read six different newspapers this morning. They are provided for free in the transit lounge.'

Friday reached into her bag and pulled out six folded newspapers.

'All of them, even the English language papers, feature a story about a priceless jade necklace that was stolen from your embassy in Geneva last night. The necklace was originally looted from China during the Opium Wars of the nineteenth century. Your ambassador was going to present it to the Chinese ambassador at a formal dinner this evening as a

14

gesture of goodwill to a growing trade partner,' said Friday. 'It's not a secret. It's news.'

'I'm not discussing it with you,' said Mr Quigley.

'Why not?' said Friday. 'What have you got to lose? I'm not going to tell anyone. I can't even leave the airport. And if I did tell someone, no one would believe me because I'm just a twelve-year-old girl.'

'Let's just fill out your paperwork and I can begin trying to process it,' said Mr Quigley, taking a set of forms out of his briefcase. 'We've located your parents now. They're at a university in Estonia. Once we have all your information, we'll get them to fill out the forms.'

'If you do find them, you'll never get them to fill out the forms,' said Friday. 'Certainly not properly. They couldn't even give my name to the birth registrar. It would be much better if you simply issued me with an exigent circumstances passport.'

'We can't do that,' said Mr Quigley. 'That's only for the most exceptional circumstances, for political refugees and defectors.'

'I am exceptional,' said Friday.

'You're certainly not exceptionally modest,' said Mr Quigley with raised eyebrows.

15

'I'll prove it to you,' said Friday. 'I'll find the necklace.'

'You're not allowed to leave the airport transit lounge,' said Mr Quigley.

'That will be the bit that proves I'm exceptional,' said Friday with a smile.

'I haven't got time for this,' said Mr Quigley, reflexively glancing at his phone even though it was turned off.

'Really?' said Friday. 'You haven't got time for a fifteen-minute conversation with me that could result in you finding the necklace as soon as you get back to Geneva?'

Mr Quigley hesitated. He was clearly warring with himself.

'I've solved bank robberies, thwarted smuggling operations and uncovered escaped convicts,' said Friday. 'Your problem is well within my skill set.'

Mr Quigley sighed. 'You're not going to shut up until we do this, are you?'

'No,' agreed Friday happily.

Chapter 3

▰▰▰▰▰▰▰▰▰▰▰▰▰▰▰

The Case of the Stolen Necklace

'All right, tell me where the necklace is,' said Mr Quigley unenthusiastically.

'I'll need to ask you a few questions first,' said Friday. 'Who are your suspects?'

'We don't have any,' said Mr Quigley with a shrug. 'We've got no idea how the thief broke in.'

'They can't have broken in,' said Friday. 'Embassies have the highest level of security. It would be impossible to break in without leaving some evidence, a scratched lock, a shadowy figure on security footage, a dusty footprint, something like that. It must have been an inside job.'

'How dare you!' exclaimed Mr Quigley. 'Embassy staff are hand-picked for their honesty and integrity.'

'Please,' said Friday. 'You've admitted you talk on the phone while you're driving, so you've already demonstrated moral flexibility. Just tell me, who was in the embassy?'

'I can't tell you that,' said Mr Quigley.

'Okay,' said Friday, 'I'll work it out. I know from the paper that the Ambassador has a wife and two teenage children. The necklace was stolen at night, so there would be none of the day staff, just some security guards and servants.'

'There are no live-in servants,' said Mr Quigley. 'This isn't the nineteenth century.'

'There would be a few officials on the night desk. They are on call 24/7,' said Friday. 'An embassy always needs to be able to react to events. So someone would be on duty to inform the Ambassador if he had to launch into action.'

'It can't have been any of them,' said Mr Quigley, shaking his head. 'The necklace was stored in a special high-security display room in the residence.'

'Tell me about the room,' said Friday. 'What security measures were in place?'

'The room is the most secure place in the embassy. There are no windows, air conditioning vents or under-floor access points. There is no way in, except through the door,' said Mr Quigley.

'Tell me about the door and the locks,' said Friday.

'It's a ten-foot-high steel-lined double door with a titanium frame bolted into the stone walls,' said Mr Quigley. 'It has two sets of deadlocks. One at ground level and the other at the top of the door.'

'I see,' said Friday. 'So you need a key to lock or unlock the door?'

'The display room is in the domestic quarters,' continued Mr Quigley, 'and at night that area is entirely sealed off from the embassy offices, in case there is some sort of political attack.'

'So it was just the family in the domestic quarters?' asked Friday.

'No, the Ambassador had taken his family skiing for the weekend. The only person in the domestic area was the chef,' said Mr Quigley. 'He was working through the night making a huge ice sculpture and a blackforest cherry cake for the big black-tie dinner.

He heard a noise coming from the display room and went to investigate.'

'I see, and according to the papers the chef was assaulted by the thief,' said Friday.

'Yes, we haven't been able to get much sense out of him,' said Mr Quigley. 'He had a big lump on the back of his head, and he's in hospital being treated for hypothermia.'

'How did he get hypothermia?' asked Friday.

'He was soaking wet when we found him,' said Mr Quigley. 'His clothes were completely drenched. The thief locked him in the display room so he couldn't raise the alarm.'

'Did the chef have a key to the display room?' asked Friday.

'Yes, it was still on him when we found him,' said Mr Quigley.

'So if he had regained consciousness, he could have let himself out,' said Friday.

'No,' said Mr Quigley, 'because he would have had no way of reaching the lock at the top of the ten-foot-tall door.'

'Ahh,' said Friday. 'The classic closed-room conundrum.'

'Huh? Has living in the airport affected your mental health?' said Mr Quigley, starting to look optimistic. 'If it has, that's great, I can use that to get you released into a hospital. Admittedly, a mental hospital, but it might do you some good.'

'The answer lies with the missing ice sculpture,' said Friday.

'What?' said Mr Quigley.

'You mentioned it earlier when you were talking on the phone,' said Friday. 'An ice sculpture has gone missing from the embassy.'

'Yes, but I don't see what that's got to do with anything,' said Mr Quigley. He was looking thoroughly confused.

'Which is exactly what the thief wanted you to think,' said Friday, 'or, rather, not think. Because that's what the thief wanted – for you to not think about the ice sculpture.'

'So where is the ice sculpture?' asked Mr Quigley.

'Oh, you'll never find it,' said Friday.

'Are you trying to irritate me?' asked Mr Quigley.

'It melted after it was used by the thief,' said Friday.

Mr Quigley stood up. 'I'll write to your parents. You're being purposefully obstructive. I can't deal with you.'

'The necklace was stolen by the chef,' said Friday. 'He was the only person with the opportunity to commit the crime, so he had to divert suspicion away from himself. After he stole the necklace, he hid it somewhere in the kitchen. Then he locked himself in the display room, and gave himself a bang on the head to make the whole thing believable.'

'But that's impossible,' said Mr Quigley. 'There is no way the chef could have locked the door from the inside, not without a ladder. And there was no ladder in the room.'

'Ah, but there was a four-foot-tall ice statue,' said Friday. 'The chef slid that into the room, stood on it to lock himself in, then waited for the sculpture to melt. Once it was nothing more than a puddle, he rolled in the water to hide the evidence. Hence the hypothermia.'

'I suppose it's possible,' said Mr Quigley. 'But it's also ridiculous. It's impossible to prove.'

'Not when you find the necklace,' said Friday.

'You can't know where that is,' said Mr Quigley.

'But I do,' said Friday. 'With the necklace stolen, the chef knew that the embassy would be searched. He needed to hide it somewhere no one would look.'

'Please don't tell me he swallowed it,' said Mr Quigley.

'No, but you're thinking along the right lines,' said Friday. 'He hid it in the cake.'

'That's crazy,' said Mr Quigley.

'Not at all,' said Friday. 'With the necklace gone, the chef knew the dinner would be cancelled. No one would want the cake. It would be his to dispose of as he chose.'

'The whole scenario is far-fetched,' said Mr Quigley.

'It is,' agreed Friday. 'But it is the only scenario that fits the facts; therefore, ridiculous as it is, that's what happened.'

Mr Quigley looked at her.

'If I were you,' continued Friday, 'I'd turn my phone back on now, call the embassy and ask the head of security to look in that cake.'

Mr Quigley considered the situation.

'Or you could ignore my advice and let the chef dispose of the cake,' said Friday. 'I'll bet he says something virtuous, like he's going to donate it to a homeless shelter or something. The great thing is, because Switzerland is such a small country, he can have it across the border in a couple of hours.'

Mr Quigley grabbed his phone and started dialling. 'Roberts, there's a giant blackforest cherry cake in the kitchen. I need you to search the cake. You heard me, look inside the cake for the necklace. I don't care. Use your hands if you have to.'

Two minutes later the head of security came back on the phone. The necklace was found. The chef had hidden it in the creamy filling between the third and fourth layers of sponge.

An international crisis had been averted.

After 45 minutes of filling in forms and copying documents, Friday was handed a brand new passport.

'Congratulations, you are now a citizen,' said Mr Quigley, shaking her hand.

Friday had never been so relieved to hold a document. The cover was still neat and crisp, and had gold embossing. She opened it up to the photograph page. The photo of her was predictably awful. It was the one Interpol had taken when she had tried to enter Switzerland without any papers.

'Hey, it's made out to Freitag Scheunen!' said Friday.

'That's your name,' said Mr Quigley.

'Only officially,' said Friday.

'We're a government agency,' said Mr Quigley. 'We only do things officially. If you want to change your name, you will have to contact the appropriate authorities and fill in the necessary paperwork when you get home.'

'But I'm twelve,' said Friday. 'My parents are going to have to sign the forms. It will take me forever to get hold of them to do that.'

'I can't solve all your problems,' said Mr Quigley. 'I've just rescued you from living in an airport. That will have to be enough for today. The embassy will book you a flight home. We'll bill your parents for it later.'

'No need,' said Friday, pulling her wallet out of her pocket. It was bulging with cash of all different denominations. 'I'll sort it out myself. The lady at the Lufthansa desk owes me a favour. I've been coaching her in economic theory to help her pass the MBA admissions exam. If I book a flight with her, she'll be able to get me an upgrade to business class.'

'I'm glad you'll soon be on home soil,' said Mr Quigley. 'Switzerland's loss is our gain.'

Chapter 4

▪▪▪▪▪▪▪▪▪▪▪▪▪▪▪▪▪▪▪▪▪▪

The Return

When Friday stepped through customs into the arrivals hall, she was immediately grabbed in a total body lock. That's what it felt like getting a bear hug from someone as big as Uncle Bernie.

'I'm so glad you're home,' said Uncle Bernie.

'Me too,' said Friday.

'I was so worried,' said Uncle Bernie. 'And it was all my fault. When those immigration officials came to your school, I should have tackled them and given you a chance to make a run for it.'

'It's best you didn't,' said Friday. 'You would have got in trouble. And I'm terrible at running, so it never would have worked.'

'Now that you've got your freedom, what do you want to do first?' asked Uncle Bernie.

'Go to school,' said Friday.

'You don't want to celebrate by going to a fun park or having a day at the beach?' asked Uncle Bernie.

'Come on, this is me,' said Friday. 'School is my idea of a fun park.'

'All right,' said Uncle Bernie, shaking his head. 'I suppose you're worried about being three weeks behind on the coursework.'

'Of course not,' said Friday. 'The coursework is a doddle. Except for PE – that's cruel and unusual torture. I just want to get back to the school. International airports are interesting, but when it comes to a hotbed of human conflict, greed, jealousy and crime you can't beat Highcrest Academy. I think it's all the hormones in the teenagers. They live their lives on a higher level of drama than normal people.'

Two hours later, Uncle Bernie and Friday pulled into the driveway of Highcrest Academy. It was 10 o'clock on a Wednesday morning. Normally you would expect to see students playing cricket or doing rugby drills on the sports fields, or drive past a biology class being forced to observe the fauna in a clump of bushes. But there was no one about.

'It seems oddly quiet,' said Friday.

'Maybe they're having a school assembly,' said Uncle Bernie.

'On a Wednesday?' said Friday. 'Don't be ridiculous. Mrs Marigold serves pancakes for breakfast on Wednesdays, so by 10 o'clock in the morning the Headmaster will be asleep in the armchair in his office. Carbohydrates have that effect on him. There's no way he'd interrupt that for an assembly.'

Uncle Bernie parked at the top of the driveway.

'Are you sure it's okay if I just drop you off?' said Uncle Bernie. 'Your school gives me the heebie-jeebies. It's like travelling back in time to a boarding school in a Dickens novel. But this time it's weirdly quiet.'

At that moment there was a roar of cheers from a distant crowd.

'What was that?' asked Uncle Bernie.

'It sounded like a football crowd,' said Friday. 'So there must be plenty of people here. I'll be fine. You've got to get back to work.'

Friday hugged Uncle Bernie and waved goodbye, then walked past the administration building toward the school quadrangle.

When she got there it was a shocking sight. Instead of seeing the ordered progress of students going about their day, there was total chaos. The students were dressed like savages.

There was no school uniform at Highcrest Academy, but there was a dress code. Boys were meant to wear collared shirts, and on their bodies, not wrapped around their heads. Shoes were meant to be worn on feet, not used as projectiles hurled at fleeing year 7 students. And many of the students seemed to be wearing a mimicry of tribal war paint.

In the centre of the quadrangle was the most bizarre thing of all.

Two huge catapults had been constructed. One was loaded with an overhead projector, while the other was being loaded with a three-drawer filing cabinet by Lizzie and Max Abercrombie. Friday had not had much to do with the twins who were in year 9, because they were good-looking and athletic, so she didn't have much in common with them.

'Are you ready?!'

Friday looked across to see Ian Wainscott holding onto the flagpole and hanging a metre off the ground by balancing his weight on the rope hook. The crowd turned to him, hungry for his leadership.

Friday was thoroughly shocked by the anarchy of the situation. But a small part of her brain was still able to register that Ian looked very attractive without his shirt on. His athletic frame, low body fat ratio and swimmer's tan combined to create an appealing effect. At least, that's how Friday's brain interpreted what her hormones were telling her.

'Thank goodness you're back!'

Friday turned to be enveloped in her second big hug of the day. It was Melanie Pelly, her best friend.

'Don't ever leave me again,' said Melanie.

'That's a bit strong,' said Friday, releasing herself from Melanie's grip. 'You can cope without me. You were here for a year before I started.'

'I know I can cope,' said Melanie, 'but I don't want to. Things are so much easier when you're here to make sure I don't lock myself out of our room, give me all the answers to the homework questions and remind me which lesson we're sitting in.'

'What happened?' asked Friday, turning back to the scene in the quadrangle. 'I've only been gone three weeks. How did the school end up like this?'

'Everything was the same as usual for two weeks and six days,' said Melanie. 'Except you weren't here, so I had to go to all my classes, which was exhausting. Things were a little dull, really. Then, on Monday, everything exploded.'

'Literally?' asked Friday. She enjoyed weapons-grade explosives as much as the next curious-minded pre-teen, and she would have been disappointed to miss a large blast.

'No, emotionally,' said Melanie. 'The teachers all received letters telling them they had been fired.'

'The Headmaster fired everyone?!' said Friday.

'No, the letters came from the school council,' said Melanie. 'They said that because of the school's ongoing descent into shambolic academic inept-itude, they were going to hire an entirely new teaching staff.'

'So the school has been without teachers for twenty-four hours?' said Friday.

'Worse than that,' said Melanie. 'There's no cook. Mrs Marigold was fired, too. We've been reduced to foraging in the vegetable garden and fishing in the swamp.'

'Why didn't you just order pizza?' asked Friday.

'We did at first, but the pizza shop in town refuses to deliver anymore,' said Melanie. 'They made the mistake of sending out their cutest delivery boy. He never stood a chance.'

'But what is the Headmaster doing about all this?' asked Friday. 'Why has he let this happen?'

'BARNES!'

Friday turned around to see the Headmaster yelling at her from the window of the administration building.

'Get in here, I need to talk to you,' said the Headmaster. He slammed the window quickly before it was showered with a volley of mud thrown by the students below.

When Friday and Melanie reached the door of the administration building, it was locked.

'Let me in!' called Friday.

'Can't, I'm not allowed to open the door for anyone except Friday Barnes,' said a familiar voice.

'Binky, is that you?' asked Friday.

'Yes,' said Binky. 'Is that you, Friday? Or someone pretending to be you?'

'Why on earth would anyone pretend to be me?' asked Friday.

'Word got out that the Headmaster has a large supply of chocolate biscuits in the admin block,' said Binky. 'Mirabella Peterson has been doing increasingly desperate things to try to get in here.'

'It's really Friday,' said Melanie. 'Let us in.'

'Melanie, is that you?' asked Binky.

Binky was Melanie's brother, so he really should have recognised her voice, but his strength did not lie in thinking. But he was very tall and strong, so he was the person to go to if you needed a door guarded against a horde of chocolate-starved girls.

'Just let us in,' ordered Melanie.

The door unlocked and Binky peeked around the side. 'I'm so glad to see you,' said Binky. 'I don't like having this kind of responsibility.'

'Why isn't Debbie with you?' asked Friday.

'When the riot broke out, her father had her airlifted back to Norway,' said Binky.

'I'm so sorry,' said Friday.

'It's all right,' said Binky. 'I've started learning Norwegian. As soon as I finish school, I'm going to go to Norway and win her back.'

'Bra for deg,' said Friday.

'What?' said Binky.

'I said "good for you" in Norwegian,' said Friday.

'Oh, I haven't got that far,' said Binky. 'I can only say "yes" and "sorry".'

'Not yes and no?' asked Friday.

'No,' said Binky. 'Saying "no" sounds rude.'

'Barnes, get in here!' said the Headmaster. He was standing in the doorway to his office.

Friday and Melanie followed him in and he slammed the door shut behind them.

'Why did you fire all the teachers?' asked Friday.

'I didn't,' said the Headmaster.

'Okay, why did the school council fire all the teachers?' asked Friday.

'They didn't, either,' said the Headmaster.

'But what about the letters the teachers received?' asked Friday.

'They were forgeries,' said the Headmaster.

'Really?' said Friday. 'If someone was that good at forging things, why would they forge termination letters? Surely forging bond certificates would be a more efficient use of their time.'

'I can't fathom the motives behind why the crazy students and staff do the things they do,' said the Headmaster. 'I just wish they would stop it and go back to blowing spitballs and stealing mascots like at normal schools.'

'Can't you call the teachers and explain?' asked Friday.

'I've tried,' said the Headmaster. 'But the termination letters are so specific they don't believe me. They're not just form letters. They give detailed accounts of all the teachers' failings.'

'Like Mr Atwood's drinking problem?' asked Melanie.

'I didn't know that Mr Atwood had a drinking problem!' exclaimed the Headmaster.

'I'm sure he doesn't,' said Melanie. 'I must have misunderstood. He probably has a persistent cough and that's why he keeps having to pretend he dropped a pencil and take sips from a bottle under his desk.'

'No, Mr Atwood's letter accused him of being a bigamist,' said the Headmaster.

'That sounds a bit far-fetched,' said Friday. 'How could anybody afford to have two wives on a teacher's salary?'

'He's actually got three wives and they are all extremely successful business executives,' said the Headmaster.

'Ah,' said Melanie, 'no wonder he has to drink. It must be exhausting not getting their names wrong.'

'It turns out several staff members have criminal records,' said the Headmaster.

'Really?' said Friday. 'Who?'

'Mr Davies has a juvenile conviction for using illegal explosives,' said the Headmaster. 'Apparently, when he was nine years old, he submitted a model of a volcano to his school science fair and he used something more powerful than baking soda and vinegar in his explosion.'

'Who else?' asked Melanie.

'Mrs Cannon,' said the Headmaster.

'That doesn't surprise me,' said Friday.

'She has a conviction for espionage,' said the Head-master. 'It appears that when she was nineteen she travelled with a dance troupe to Cuba. Fidel Castro caught her performance at a local club and invited her to dinner, where she gave a detailed analysis of the causes of the economic problems in the Western world. Her defence was she was just making small talk.'

'And the forger knew all this,' said Friday.

'Their information was impeccable,' said the Headmaster.

'And exhaustive,' said Friday. 'It would take an enormous amount of research to dig up dirt on every teacher in the school.'

'I need you to find out who it is,' said the Headmaster.

'Can you show me one of the letters?' asked Friday.

'No, I don't have copies,' said the Headmaster. 'You'll have to go and see the teachers.'

'Where are they?' asked Friday.

'Most of them have gone home,' said the Headmaster. 'But a few stalwarts have taken up residence in town at the pub.'

'If you give us a lift into town we'll talk to them,' said Friday.

'Can't you ride a bicycle?' asked the Headmaster. 'Last time I went into town they egged my car.'

'All right,' said Friday. 'But bicycle-riding will increase my fee.'

'Your fee?!' exclaimed the Headmaster. 'Where is your school pride? Won't you do this for Highcrest Academy?'

'I'll do it for one semester of free board and tuition,' said Friday. 'That'll have me paid up until halfway through next year.'

'How can I be expected to run a school if I give board and tuition away?' asked the Headmaster.

'If you don't get your teachers back, you won't have a school,' said Friday. 'So not paying me would be a false economy.'

'All right, I agree to your terms. Get going, then,' said the Headmaster.

'You're forgetting something,' said Friday.

'I am?' asked the Headmaster.

'You need to lend us a bicycle,' said Friday.

Chapter 5

▰▰▰▰▰▰▰▰▰▰▰▰▰▰▰▰▰

In Town

It turned out that the only bicycle at the school was a 1950s tandem cruiser, which was probably a good thing because there was no way Melanie had any intention of doing any pedalling. Luckily, the town was only five kilometres away and most of the journey was downhill, so it took Friday and Melanie an hour and a half to get there. This may seem like a long time to cycle five kilometres, but they did fall off twice. The second time they punctured a tyre and Melanie fell asleep in the grass while Friday was changing the inner tube. Then it took some time for Friday to wake Melanie up enough for her to be able to balance in her seat.

When they finally rolled into town Friday was sweaty, dirty and very scratched up. Somehow, despite sleeping in a ditch and falling off a bicycle twice, Melanie managed to look relaxed and well presented.

'There are the teachers,' said Friday.

Several members of the teaching staff were sitting in the beer garden out the front of the pub. It was a beautiful sunny day. The pub looked very hospitable. Although Mr Maclean had taken his shirt off and was sunbathing.

'Ew,' said Melanie.

'I know,' said Friday. 'Remind me to report him to the police before we go back.'

'Hello!' called Mrs Cannon, waving to the girls. 'Have you come for a chat? Let me buy you both an orange juice.'

'This isn't a social call,' said Friday. 'The Headmaster has hired me to investigate the forged termination letters.'

'Ha!' said Mrs Cannon. 'He's still using that excuse, is he?'

'It's not my fault I have ringworm!' declared Mr Maclean. 'My union representative says it's not grounds for termination.'

'My name is Mrs Cannon,' said Mrs Cannon. 'Stop calling me "your union representative". It makes me sound like I'm concerned for your welfare, and I can assure you I'm not.'

'*You're* the union representative?' asked Friday.

'I am,' said Mrs Cannon.

'But you hate doing things,' said Melanie.

'I know,' said Mrs Cannon. 'Which is why I care so passionately about the union movement. The only thing that galvanises me into action is when someone wants me to do more work.'

'Have you got one of the termination letters?' asked Friday. 'Perhaps it holds a clue.'

'I'm reluctant to show them to you, girls,' said Mrs Cannon. 'They are all deeply personal, offensive and dangerously truthful. Who knew the staff at Highcrest Academy had done so many dreadful things in the past?'

'I didn't mean to poison the Indonesian ambassador,' said Mrs Marigold, the school cook, bursting into tears.

The tears shocked Friday and Melanie more than the revelation that the school cook had poisoned someone. Mrs Marigold was such a battleaxe and it took a lot to rattle her.

'There there, dear,' said Mrs Cannon. 'No one blames you. If they are going to sell rat poison in boxes the same size and shape as sea salt, what can they expect?'

'Besides, it only qualifies you more for cooking at Highcrest,' said Mr Maclean. 'There are so many students who deserve to be poisoned.'

'Mr Maclean, shame on you! Threatening a culinary assault on children will not help our cause,' said Mrs Cannon. 'Putting your shirt back on might, though.'

'There must be one letter we can look at,' said Friday.

'I suppose you can look at mine,' said Mrs Cannon. 'The accusations of espionage have all been a matter of public record, anyway. If anything, the letter is a sad reflection on the former headmaster's ability to do background checks. But I was very thin and pretty thirty years ago, so I can't blame him for his high opinion of my other assets.' Mrs Cannon reached into her handbag and pulled out a pink sheet of paper.

'At least they used pretty stationery,' said Melanie. 'It's traditional for termination letters to be printed on pink paper,' said Friday.

'It's helpful, really,' said Mrs Cannon. 'It saves you from having to read the letter. You can just start crying as soon as you see the colour of the paper. Although, of course, it can make Valentine's Day very awkward.'

Friday scanned the letter. 'It all looks very straightforward,' she said. 'Apart from the shocking details of your sordid past, this is a perfectly formal standard termination letter.'

'The stationery looks authentic,' said Melanie. 'With the school crest embossed in the letterhead.'

Friday ran her hand over the raised print.

'Someone could have stolen the stationery,' said Melanie.

'The school council wouldn't have had sixty sheets of pink letterhead,' said Friday. 'They would have had to get it printed specially.' She held the sheet of paper up so the sun shone through it.

'What are you looking for?' asked Melanie.

'Watermarks,' said Friday. 'All good-quality

stationery has a semi-transparent watermark made into the paper. Oh dear . . .'

'What is it?' said Mrs Cannon.

'I can't tell exactly,' said Friday, 'because the passage about you teaching Fidel Castro the lambada is obscuring the picture. Mr Maclean, show me your letter.'

'I will not,' said Mr Maclean. 'It is very rude.'

'Show her your letter,' said Mrs Cannon, 'or I'll tell her about the time you nearly got fired for skinny-dipping in the swamp.'

'That's a breach of confidentiality!' protested Mr Maclean. 'Besides, I was not skinny-dipping. I had my underwear on. I just didn't want to get my chinos wet when I was caught out by rising tidewater on the far side of the swamp.'

'That's what they all say,' said Mrs Cannon, grabbing Mr Maclean's shirt from the back of the chair it hung on and fishing the letter out of the top pocket.

'Hey!' yelled Mr Maclean.

'That will serve you right for sunbathing in a public place while people are trying to keep their breakfast down,' said Mrs Cannon, handing the letter over to Friday.

Friday held up Mr Maclean's letter. The water-mark was clearer in this one.

'Can you see anything?' asked Melanie.

'Yes,' said Friday. 'A face.'

'Really?' said Melanie.

'Take a look,' said Friday. 'Does it remind you of anyone?'

Melanie looked at the watermark.

'Beautiful smile, piercing eyes, floppy hair – it looks like . . . Ian!' said Melanie.

'And can you read the writing beneath?' said Friday.

'*Ego omnes seducti estis*?' said Melanie. 'What does that mean?'

'It's Latin,' said Friday. 'It means, "I fooled you all".'

'Oh, Ian,' said Melanie. 'So this means he's the one who forged the letters?'

'I can't believe he would do something so large-scale,' said Friday.

'Well, that's because you weren't here,' said Melanie. 'You didn't see how lost he was without you.'

'Don't start that again,' said Friday.

45

'He missed you dreadfully,' said Melanie. 'He barely said anything sarcastic. And when he did, none of us were smart enough to understand what he was talking about. He must have cooked all this up for fun.'

'He certainly seemed to be enjoying the catapult back at the school,' said Friday, 'but this seems too cruel for him.'

Melanie put her arm around Friday. 'That's because you love him, so you are blind to his weaknesses.'

'Just like me and Fidel,' said Mrs Cannon.

'You loved Fidel Castro?' asked Friday.

'No, *he* was in love with *me*,' said Mrs Cannon. 'Just because he's a communist dictator, doesn't mean he can't have good taste in ladies.'

'I suppose I'll have to tell the Headmaster,' said Friday glumly.

'No need,' said Mr Maclean, tucking his mobile phone into his trouser pocket. 'I just texted him what you uncovered. I told him we would all be ready to resume work first thing tomorrow.'

'You are such a goody-two-shoes,' said Mrs Cannon.

'We'd better get back to the school,' said Friday, 'before the Headmaster overreacts. I'm sure there must be more to this.'

Melanie and Friday jumped back on their bicycle and hurried back to the school as fast as they could. Unfortunately this was not terribly fast. Going back was mainly uphill. And their legs were tired from the downhill ride into town. It was two hours before they cycled painstakingly slowly up the gravel driveway to the administration building, lumbered off the bicycle and staggered inside to confront the Headmaster.

Chapter 6

The Bitter Farewell

'Headmaster,' said Friday, struggling for breath, 'you mustn't overreact.'

'How dare you barge into my office!' barked the Headmaster. 'Just because you're in here all the time from causing trouble, doesn't mean you can waltz in whenever you like.'

'I think there's more to this than meets the eye,' said Friday.

'I'm very grateful to you for finding the culprit

and resolving the industrial dispute,' said the Headmaster. 'You'll get your board and tuition covered. Isn't that enough?'

'I don't believe Ian would do this,' said Friday.

'Oh, I see,' said the Headmaster. 'You didn't realise it was your boyfriend you were dropping in it.'

'He's not my boyfriend,' said Friday.

'Yes, yes,' said the Headmaster, 'you can delude yourself, but you can't expect the rest of us not to notice what we see with our own eyes.'

'My opinion is based on fact and reason,' said Friday.

'And just a little bit of warm affection,' said Melanie. 'Ian is seriously handsome. It's hard to believe someone so good-looking would do something so ugly.'

'I'm just asking you to wait while I investigate further before you take action,' said Friday.

The Headmaster sighed. 'You're too late,' he said. 'I confronted Wainscott immediately. He laughed. He didn't deny it.'

'What would be the point when there was so much evidence against him,' said Friday sadly.

'That's exactly what he said,' said the Headmaster. 'It's unnerving how simpatico you two are.'

'So you suspended him?' asked Friday.

'He sacked the entire staff two days ago!' said the Headmaster. 'Several of them have found other jobs. Some have taken off on holidays, leaving no contact details. And Vice Principal Dean was so devastated to be fired that he . . . well, that's none of your business.'

'Had a mental breakdown?' guessed Friday.

'How did you know?' asked the Headmaster.

'I didn't,' said Friday. 'But it makes sense. He was never very stable.'

'Even when the teachers come back tomorrow it will take weeks, if not months, before things return to normal,' said the Headmaster, slumping in his seat.

'What are you saying?' asked Friday, although her blood chilled as she feared the worst.

'Wainscott has been stripped of his scholarship and expelled,' said the Headmaster. 'I called a taxi for him. He packed his things and left an hour ago.'

Friday's vision began to blur and the room started to spin. She fainted.

Chapter 7

Dullness Ensues

Friday was shell-shocked for days. Melanie had long teased her about being in love with Ian Wainscott, and she had always shrugged it off as silliness. But she was beginning to suspect that her roommate might be more insightful than she'd realised.

For while she sincerely believed that she wasn't in love with Ian, there was no denying the empirical evidence. When she saw Ian, her pulse raced, her breath quickened and she became less able to speak articulately.

Friday had always reasoned that this was a normal hormonal response to seeing a good-looking boy. For there was no doubt that Ian was incredibly good-looking. But she could not explain her reaction now that Ian was gone. She felt malaise. Her spirits were low, her senses felt dull and usually simple tasks, such as getting out of bed in the morning, seemed to be heavy with futility.

Friday was sitting in biology, staring out the window, thinking about how heavy her eyelids felt and wondering if she could rest them one eyelid at a time without falling asleep when she realised someone was yelling at her.

'Barnes!' yelled Mr Poshoglian.

Friday turned to look at the teacher. His face was red. She couldn't imagine what he could be so angry about.

'What?' she asked.

'The function of the mitochondria in the cell?!' demanded Mr Poshoglian.

'Really?' said Friday. 'You're a biology teacher and you don't know?'

'Of course I know!' exclaimed Mr Poshoglian, 'I'm asking if *you* know.'

'Yes,' said Friday.

'Then what is it?' yelled Mr Poshoglian. He was getting seriously agitated that his one student who knew anything seemed to have contracted a sudden bout of extreme ignorance.

'Sorry, what was the question again?' asked Friday.

'It converts ATP to ADP, providing energy on a cellular level,' said Melanie (with Friday so distracted, there had been a role reversal in their relationship and Melanie had been paying attention in class). 'And you'll have to excuse Friday, sir. She's never suffered heartbreak before, and she's taking it very badly.'

'I'm not suffering heartbreak,' protested Friday.

'You see, she's still in denial,' said Melanie. 'She's got a long way to go in the grieving process.'

'I'm not suffering heartbreak!' yelled Friday again.

'Ah, anger,' said Melanie. 'The third stage of grieving. Let it out, Friday. I know you're not used to dealing with emotions, but it is healthier to let them out.'

'Ladies!' snapped Mr Poshoglian. 'This is a biology class, not a therapy session. Save your discussions of boyfriends until after class.'

'He's not my boyfriend,' protested Friday.

'Well, of course he dumped you,' said Mirabella Peterson, one of Friday's less pleasant classmates. 'You got him expelled from school.'

'Hot boys don't like that kind of thing,' agreed Tia Babcock, knowledgably.

'He is not . . . actually he is hot,' said Friday. 'That's just a fact. I can't argue with that.'

'Right, that's it!' declared Mr Poshoglian. 'Barnes, get out! Go and see the Headmaster.'

'Good idea,' said Melanie. 'He's always got chocolate biscuits. Ask him to give you one. That will cheer you up.'

'You get out too, Pelly!' snapped Mr Poshoglian. 'I'm sick of both of you and your teen angst.'

'Friday is only twelve,' said Melanie.

'I don't care!' said Mr Poshoglian. 'Get out of my classroom. We're trying to study biology!'

'I would have thought that adolescent courtship rituals fell under the subject area of biology,' said Melanie as she packed up her books.

'Get out!' yelled Mr Poshoglian.

'Mr Posh,' said Melanie, 'you're going to have an aneurysm if you don't calm down. Although I suppose that would be an instructive biology lesson as well.'

Mr Poshoglian threw his whiteboard eraser at Friday and Melanie as they left. Luckily, he was terrible at throwing and the eraser just hit the fume cupboard in the corner of the room.

'Do you want to talk about it?' asked Melanie as she and Friday trudged across the quadrangle.

'What?' asked Friday.

'Ian,' said Melanie.

'No,' said Friday, 'I realise I'm out of sorts, but I'm sure it's nothing to do with that. It's probably a delayed reaction to living in an airport lounge for three weeks, or discovering that I was citizenshipless. That would make more sense.'

'You keep telling yourself that,' said Melanie. 'I think you'd better stay in denial. I don't think you've got the skills to come up with a more sophisticated emotional response.'

'Huh?' said Friday. Malaise really was turning her into a dullard.

When they got to the Headmaster's office the door was closed so the girls slumped on the bench outside. Friday shut her eyes. She felt so weary. But she seemed to have lost the knack of falling asleep. She'd have to ask Melanie for a tutorial. She was an expert at instant slumber.

The Headmaster's door swung wide. Friday's eyes snapped open and she instinctively sat up so as not to be caught slouching.

But it wasn't the Headmaster who stepped out. It was a large man with wavy, greying brown hair, wearing a tie-dyed t-shirt that read 'Learning is cool!' He noticed Friday and Melanie sitting on the bench and grinned at them. There was something a little too wide-eyed and manic about his grin.

'Hello girls. You can call me VP Pete,' said the man. 'I hope you haven't been sent to the Head-master because you've been up to mischief.'

Friday stared into the man's eyes, then looked down at the sandals on his feet, before systematically inspecting him from the ground, back up to the top of his head.

'You must be the new vice principal,' said Friday.

He flinched ever so slightly.

'He doesn't look like a vice principal,' said Melanie.

'On the contrary,' said Friday. 'He's not wearing a visitor's badge, so he must be a member of staff. He can't be a regular teacher because he seems too happy and jovial. Teachers usually exude a sense of oppression. And he has the chipper disposition of a man in a position to bully others. Everything about him speaks of lower middle management.'

'But the tie-dyed t-shirt?' said Melanie.

'I imagine the Headmaster did not have a lot of choice,' said Friday. 'Vice principals aren't usually available at a moment's notice. He would have been forced to hire someone with progressive educational theories.'

VP Pete laughed. 'Traditional educational theories haven't been working well for this school, have they? I'm going to introduce some new, exciting teaching techniques and rebuild Highcrest Academy to make it a safe and supportive environment.'

'He's going to knock the buildings down and rebuild them?' asked Melanie.

'I suspect he will start out rebuilding in the figurative sense,' said Friday. 'Before he actually gets into bricklaying.'

'I'm going to rebuild your minds,' said VP Pete. 'Education these days needs to be about emotional intelligence, linear thinking and resilience.'

'Good luck with that,' said Friday. 'I hope you find your own personal transition from unemployment to school administration to be a smooth one.'

'I beg your pardon?' said VP Pete, his warm smile growing slightly chillier.

'You've clearly been unemployed for some time,' said Friday. 'You have no muscle tone in your lower back and legs, which is symptomatic of a man who watches television for ten to twelve hours per day. You are extremely pale, which is consistent with never leaving the house, although you are marginally less pale on the left side of your face, suggesting that your living room has a window to the right of the television. This also explains why you haven't entirely succumbed to rickets, as you have been getting some sunlight on your skin. And the skin on your feet is a strange blue colour. You clearly have terrible circulation. No classroom teacher has that problem, because they spend so much time standing on their feet. Also, you're above the healthy weight range for a man of your height and, statistically, unemployed people are prone to eating high-calorie food to cheer themselves up, specifically chocolate.'

'Are you usually this challenging of authority?' asked VP Pete, rapidly resembling a hippie less and less.

'Yes, she is usually rude,' said Melanie, 'but she doesn't mean to be. She's just stating facts. She doesn't realise that the truth is often socially unpalatable.'

'Well, you're wrong on the last point,' said VP Pete. 'I never eat chocolate. Dairy doesn't agree with me.'

'Ah, too much cake and biscuits, then,' said Friday. She'd clearly guessed right this time, because VP Pete blushed red with anger.

Another man bustled out of the office, and as he hurried around VP Pete he bumped straight into Friday, knocking her over.

'What are you doing there?' asked the man. He was the same height and colouring as VP Pete, but he was much thinner. He seemed very angry.

'I was just standing,' said Friday, picking herself up from the ground.

'Hello, Mr Abercrombie,' said Melanie. 'Friday, this is Lizzie and Max Abercrombie's dad. He's the president of the school council.'

'So you're Friday Barnes?' snapped Mr Abercrombie. 'Well, you're exactly what's wrong with this school. You're not going to get away with your behaviour any longer.'

'What behaviour?' asked Friday. 'My intelligence? My helpfulness?'

'Don't try to play your clever word games with me,' said Mr Abercrombie. 'I'm keeping a close eye over what happens at this school from now on. I'll be watching you. We've finally got rid of that Wainscott menace –'

'Ian?' asked Friday. 'I wouldn't have thought a man in your position would even know about him.'

'Oh, I know about that boy,' said Mr Abercrombie. 'His father was a member of the school council. It was only after he went to jail that we realised he'd defrauded us of $50,000 by claiming he would arrange to have the gym repainted, when really all he did was clean it with a high-pressure hose.'

'And you didn't notice right away?' asked Friday. 'Wasn't the lack of fresh paint a clue?'

'That's not the point!' said Mr Abercrombie. 'The point is the apple doesn't fall far from the tree. We're better off without his kind. We'll be getting rid of a few more bad apples before this situation is sorted out. You mark my words.'

'I have no need to mark your words,' said Friday. 'I am perfectly capable of remembering them. Irrational tirades always stick in my mind.'

'I'm watching you,' Mr Abercrombie said menacingly before he stormed off. VP Pete went with him.

'He was really angry,' said Friday.

'He's probably still cross about having his signature forged on those termination letters,' said Melanie.

'Barnes, is that you and Pelly out there?' called the Headmaster.

'Yes, sir,' said Friday. 'Mr Poshoglian got exasperated with us and sent us to talk to you.'

'Did he?' said the Headmaster. 'He always was the vindictive type. Would you come in then? I can't wait round all day while you chit-chat.'

'Yes, sir,' said Friday, heading into the office.

'The door, Miss Pelly,' said the Headmaster.

Melanie closed the door behind her.

'So you met the president of the school council?' asked the Headmaster.

'Yes, he seemed to have a lot of anger issues,' observed Friday.

'Do-gooders always do,' said the Headmaster. 'Highcrest Academy isn't the only institution he graces with his organisational zeal. He's chairman or treasurer of half a dozen charities and boards.'

'And we met VP Pete,' said Friday.

'Yes, our newest member of staff,' said the Headmaster. 'The school council has forced me to appoint him.'

'Yes,' said Friday, 'I worked that out.'

'VP Pete didn't like it,' said Melanie. 'I don't think he appreciates Friday's brand of deductive reasoning.'

'What did you say?' asked the Headmaster, sighing.

'Nothing,' said Friday.

'You analysed his employment status based on the colour of his feet,' Melanie reminded her.

'And that's offensive?' asked Friday.

'Most people don't like having their feet observed,' explained Melanie.

'This is exactly what I didn't want,' said the Headmaster. 'I need you to stay away from him. To stop causing trouble.'

'I never cause trouble,' protested Friday.

'Ha!' said the Headmaster. 'Whenever there's trouble, you're right there.'

'That's only because you always ask me to fix it for you,' said Friday.

'Whatever the reason, I need you to stop it,' said the Headmaster. 'I need you to keep your head down.'

'She's unusually short for her age,' said Melanie. 'How much lower can you expect her head to go?'

'Friday, now don't let this go to your ego,' said the Headmaster. 'But I need you. I rely on you to help me with this incredibly difficult-to-manage student body. Which is why I don't want you to do anything that might get you expelled.'

'I never do anything that would get me expelled,' protested Friday.

'You snuck out searching for a swamp yeti, covered up for a Norwegian princess, and went orienteering with a prison escapee,' the Headmaster reminded her.

'Technically,' conceded Friday.

'I'm on my last warning here,' said the Headmaster. 'The school council is longing for an excuse to fire me. If the school degenerates into chaos again, they might close it down entirely.'

'Surely they can't?' said Friday.

'They can and they will,' said the Headmaster. 'There are too many developers and venture capitalists on the school council. The beautifully manicured grounds, heritage-listed buildings and natural wildlife would make this the perfect location for a golf resort.'

'But this is where their children go to school,' said Friday.

'Very few of them still have children at the school,' said the Headmaster. 'Besides, they are the types who would sell their children and their grandmothers for a slice of a major development deal.'

'So they've forced you to hire VP Pete?' said Friday.

'Yes, they're making me work with a new age hippie because they're trying to break my will,' said the Headmaster.

'By exposing you to new educational theories?' said Melanie.

'I don't need new theories,' said the Headmaster. 'I've had forty years of educational reality. And the reality is that children, particularly the entitled, spoiled brats at this school, are nasty, selfish, devious little pieces of work and they don't need hand-holding or to have their emotions explored. They need some short sharp punishment, which I'm not allowed to dole out anymore because heaven forbid their massively overblown self-esteems should take the slightest dent.'

'You should write that up and put it in the prospectus,' said Friday.

'Yes, well, that just goes to show the strain I'm under,' said the Headmaster, rubbing his forehead. 'I've started speaking the truth, which will never do for a man in my line of work.'

'Evidently,' agreed Friday.

'So I want you to behave,' said the Headmaster.

'Behave in what way?' asked Friday.

'Like a stick insect,' said the Headmaster. 'For the next ten weeks, while I'm on professional probation for the debacle of the sackings, I want you to be so inactive that you go completely unnoticed.'

'I'll try my best,' said Friday.

'No, I want you to do far better than your best,' said the Headmaster. 'I've seen your best up until now and it isn't impressive. I want you to stop being yourself and do your very best impersonation of a normal student at this school.'

'There are no normal students at this school,' Melanie pointed out.

'There are a great deal who are more normal than you two,' said the Headmaster. 'For the next ten weeks, copy them!'

Chapter 8

The New Regime

The next morning an assembly had been called. Melanie was pleased because she had some of her best naps during assembly. Friday was happy too. She was going to observe the other students and see if she could get a better understanding of what 'normal' looked like. She was putting in a concerted effort. She had given up her brown cardigan, indeed all her own clothes, and was wearing an outfit of Melanie's. But it did not fit. Not just in terms of size. Melanie was a lot taller than Friday. It didn't fit her personality, either. Friday did not look right in clothes that were ironed and neatly presented.

The music started and all the students stood as the teachers paraded in from the back of the hall. The Headmaster led the way and the new vice principal followed him. VP Pete wasn't wearing tie-dye today. He was wearing a very bright floral Hawaiian shirt.

'I don't understand why I have to dress like a normal person when VP Pete doesn't,' said Friday.

'Because you're not in charge,' said Melanie.

'They should seriously think about asking me,' said Friday. 'I can handle quantum mechanics, DNA coding and Russian syntax, so school administration can't be too hard.'

'I think school administration is less about knowing the right answer and more about putting up with people,' said Melanie.

The music stopped as the teaching staff found their seats on stage.

'Good morning,' began the Headmaster. 'As you know, we have had chaos here at the school for the past few days.'

'Hurray!' cheered the more high-spirited members of the school community.

'No, "hurray" is not the correct response,' snapped the Headmaster. 'The appalling behaviour of Ian Wainscott specifically and the rest of you generally has seriously jeopardised the standing of this school.'

The students were listening now.

'Several of the teachers are threatening to sue,' continued the Headmaster. 'Two students got sprained ankles while trying to break into the kitchen, the local pizzeria has taken an apprehended violence order against all the fifth form girls, and Vice Principal Dean has been hospitalised because of the strain.'

Several students sniggered.

'This is not good!' yelled the Headmaster. 'We are now under immense scrutiny. The school council and the police will be watching everything that goes on at this school closely. Highcrest Academy has long had a tradition of mediocre academic standards, but if we degenerate into anarchy again, these official bodies will take action and close us down. Sebastian Dowell was the school's founder, and according to the terms of his will, the school can be disbanded if the student body are decided to be dangerously undisciplined.'

There was muttering in the assembly hall. Just because the students didn't try hard in their lessons did not mean they didn't have great affection for the school.

'In fact, they have already taken action,' said the Headmaster. 'They have appointed a new interim vice principal. I have been told things need to change here at Highcrest. The new vice principal will be overseeing that change.'

The Headmaster turned and went back to his seat.

VP Pete stepped up to the lectern. 'It's wonderful to be here, boys and girls. My name is Peter Dawlish, but you can call me VP Pete,' said VP Pete. 'I can't wait to get to know you all. I want you to know that I care about this school, but more importantly I care about caring, and I care about you.'

'He's lying,' observed Melanie.

'Shh,' said Friday. If she had to blend in, the least her best friend could do was to stop making outrageously accurate statements.

'This has always been a very traditional school,' continued the vice principal, 'but that clearly isn't working anymore. So things are going to change. You young people are obviously crying out for freedom. So that is what you are going to get. From now on, this school will be run on democratic principles. Every decision will be decided by vote. Students will get equal vote with teachers and senior staff.' There was muttering amongst the teachers now. 'There will be no more detention. If a student commits a transgression they will have to write a self-analysis, exploring ways in which they positively seek alternative behaviour.'

'I think I'd rather do a detention,' said Melanie.

'If you miss a class,' continued VP Pete, 'you won't have to write lines. You won't even be told off. Your punishment will be ignorance. Ignorance because you missed the fascinating lesson that your classmates enjoyed – which, in the long run, is a much greater punishment.'

'If ignorance is a punishment, then someone had better call Amnesty International,' said Friday. 'The entire student body has been brutally punished.'

'Did you have something to say, Miss Barnes?' asked VP Pete.

Everyone turned in their seats to look at Friday.

Friday was embarrassed. Her ears turned red. 'No,' said Friday.

'It's rude to talk when others are talking,' said VP Pete. 'Write me a self-analysis and have it on my desk by 9 pm tonight.'

'Okay,' said Friday.

'And make it thorough,' said VP Pete. 'I want 5000 words of really exhaustive self-examination.'

Friday decided to give up wearing normal clothes. They clearly weren't working.

Chapter 9

▰▰▰▰▰▰▰▰▰▰▰▰▰

The Case of the Missing Maths Textbooks

Later that afternoon, Friday was with Melanie in
study hall writing her self-analysis. She had actually
written well over 7000 words because she found the
subject of herself so compelling. She was just beginning an analysis of her id, when she was interrupted.

'Excuse me, Friday dear, I was wondering if you
could give me some help?'

Friday turned to see Miss Franelli, a mousy woman who looked 55 but was really only 29. Miss Franelli was a maths teacher. She loved the subject herself, but she was a kind, shy woman, so she felt dreadful for forcing children to study something that the vast majority of them loathed.

'What's the problem?' asked Friday.

'My fifth form class,' said Miss Franelli. 'All their textbooks have gone missing.'

'Where have they gone?' asked Friday.

'I don't know,' said Miss Franelli. 'I think the students have hidden them, but I've looked everywhere and I can't find them.'

'Really?' asked Friday. 'They've hidden every single textbook?'

'Ingenious,' said Melanie. 'I wish I'd thought of that.'

'They were never very enthusiastic students before,' said Miss Franelli. 'But VP Pete's talk of freedom seems to have gone to their heads.'

'Can't you report them to him?' asked Friday.

'I did,' said Miss Franelli. 'He told me that I needed to befriend the students and speak to them on their level, and if I didn't do that I'd have to look for a position at a less progressive school.'

'He can't fire you,' said Friday. 'You're the only teacher in the maths department who has a grasp of fourth-dimensional geometry.'

'I did mention that I was very qualified and that I had a master's degree in pure mathematics,' said Miss Franelli, 'but he just shook his head and said that it was this sort of patriarchal thinking that was holding back my career.'

'But what do they do in class if they're refusing to study?' asked Melanie.

'They just sit around reading romance novels,' said Miss Franelli.

'The boys as well?' asked Friday.

'Oh yes,' said Miss Franelli. 'I confronted Tristan Fanshaw about it and he told me that human relationships were the backbone of civilised society, and therefore romance novels were much more educational than anything I've taught him.'

'He probably just enjoys the kissing bits,' said Melanie.

'So what exactly happened?' asked Friday.

'Well, I had them for a double period but it was

split by recess,' said Miss Franelli. 'Before recess, they all had their textbooks. After recess, the books were gone. The students won't tell me where. I searched the classroom, the staffroom and the book closet. They weren't there. Not in any of the nearby classrooms. Not in the grounds or the gardens, or the bushes just outside the windows. I couldn't find them anywhere.'

'Perhaps they took them back to their rooms?' said Melanie.

'There wasn't time,' said Miss Franelli. 'Recess is only fifteen minutes. The senior dormitory is on the far side of the school. Besides, it was raining yesterday. They would've been soaked if they'd tried the walk. And they weren't. They were dry when they got back to class.'

'Hmm, I think I know where the textbooks are,' said Friday.

'You do?' said Miss Franelli.

'But you haven't even searched the scene of the crime,' said Melanie. 'You always search the scene of the crime, preferably with a magnifying glass and a pair of tweezers, examining every minute detail.'

'This time I just need to check the geography,' said Friday. 'Let's go and see your classroom.'

Friday, Miss Franelli and Melanie left the study hall and walked across to the school quadrangle.

'That's your classroom up there, isn't it?' asked Friday, pointing to the second-floor classroom at the end, closest to the maths staffroom.

'Yes,' said Miss Franelli.

'Then it all fits,' said Friday. 'Come on.'

When they climbed the stairs and arrived at the classroom, Miss Franelli's fifth form class were lounging around reading their novels.

'Class,' said Miss Franelli, 'Friday Barnes has come to help find your textbooks.'

'Oh good,' said Tristan Fanshaw. 'We were all so worried.'

The class sniggered at his sarcasm.

Friday scanned the room. The apathy of the senior students was palpable. They were clearly a group who spent more time styling their perfectly dishevelled hair than they did on their coursework.

'Are you going to cross-examine them?' asked Miss Franelli.

'There's not much point,' said Friday. 'They'll

just enjoy taunting me and I'd rather not give them the pleasure.' She turned and walked back to the doorway. 'Let's fetch the books.'

'Good luck with that,' called Tristan Fanshaw as Friday started walking down the corridor with Melanie and Miss Franelli.

'Where are we going?' asked Melanie.

'You said they were all entirely dry when they returned from recess,' said Friday. 'If they had stepped foot out into the rain, they would have ruined their self-consciously dishevelled hair. So, wherever they took the books, they got there by walking under-cover.'

Friday reached the end of the corridor and walked down the large staircase to the ground floor. She looked about. They were standing with the down-stairs corridor on one side, and the doorway to the quadrangle on the other. 'Now, where could they go without getting wet?'

'Along the corridor,' said Melanie.

'But then they'd be walking back towards their classroom,' said Friday. 'I think instinct would make them walk further away.'

'But it was raining outside,' said Miss Franelli.

'There is one covered walkway,' said Friday, as she stepped out into the quadrangle.

'The walkway to the library,' said Melanie.

'Precisely,' said Friday. 'A library full of books.'

'You think the textbooks are there?' asked Miss Franelli.

'I'm sure of it,' said Friday. 'What better place to hide twenty books than in a building full of tens of thousands of books.'

'We'll never find them,' said Miss Franelli.

'Don't be so sure,' said Friday. 'Let's go and see.' She walked directly across the quadrangle to the library on the far side.

Two minutes later they were standing in the romance section of the school library.

'These are all romance books,' said Miss Franelli.

'No, they just look like romance books,' said Friday. She took one down from the shelf and opened it up. 'Okay, this one actually is a romance book, but the textbooks will be here somewhere.'

Friday started taking stacks of romance novels down from the shelves.

'What are you doing?' demanded the librarian, striding over to the section.

Friday and the librarian did not get along. Given Friday's love of books you would think she would be a librarian's favourite. But the librarian at Highcrest Academy was a woman of strong views. She did not like children. She especially didn't like children who touched her books. Most of all, she didn't like impertinent children who criticised the purchases she made for the science section, which is exactly what Friday had done when they first met. Ever since, the librarian had hated Friday with the intense repressed rage only someone who works in an environment where yelling is forbidden can possess.

'We're looking for maths textbooks,' said Friday.

'You're not going to find them here,' said the librarian.

'I think I will,' said Friday. 'Miss Franelli's class left the first half of their lesson with their textbooks. When they returned they had romance novels.'

'These are not maths textbooks,' said the librarian, snatching the books away from Friday and stacking them back on the shelf. 'They are not the right size.

These are standard B4 hardbacks. Textbooks are quarto size.'

'Of course,' said Friday. 'You're right. But I don't understand. All the evidence leads to here. The textbooks must be here somewhere.'

'Do you have any quarto romance novels?' asked Melanie.

'Romance novels aren't printed in quarto,' said Friday.

'Actually,' said the librarian, 'they are when they are published in large print for the visually challenged.'

'The what?' asked Melanie.

'People with bad eyesight,' said Friday. 'But there aren't any students here who are visually impaired.'

'No,' said the librarian, 'but we did get a large collection of books donated to us by Lady Cutler. She had an excellent ornithology collection and first edition travel memoirs. But her eyesight failed in her later years and she mainly read large-print romance novels.'

'Where are they kept?' asked Friday.

'In their own section,' said the librarian. She led them to the far end of the library where two entire bookshelves were jam-packed with oversized romance novels. 'Lady Cutler was an avid reader.'

'We can see,' said Friday. She reached out and took a book from the centre shelf, then took off the dust jacket. The dust jacket read *The Sheikh's Ambitious Bride*, but when she removed it the title on the spine of the book read *Senior Mathematics, 17th edition*.

'Those little ingrates,' said the librarian, snatching down books and discovering one textbook after another. 'I let them come in here to get out of the rain, because goodness knows only meteorological intervention could possibly inspire them to read, and this is how they repay me!'

'Don't worry,' said Friday, 'Miss Franelli knows where your novels are.'

'The hard part will be getting them to give them back,' worried Miss Franelli.

'I'll get them,' said the librarian with ominous menace.

'You will?' said Miss Franelli hopefully.

'It will be my pleasure,' said the librarian as she strode off with Miss Franelli back towards the maths classroom.

The yelling could be heard from as far away as the school swamp.

'That was fun,' said Friday. 'I haven't had a good mystery to solve in ages.'

'Since Ian left,' said Melanie.

'Since I promised not to cause trouble,' said Friday. 'I can't wait for the Headmaster to get off probation so I can be a stickybeak again.'

Chapter 10

The Case of the Wet Boy

Several days later, Friday and Melanie were emerging from their history lesson where they had been studying the history of the bikini (that was what the class had democratically decided they were most interested in), when Nigel, a third form boy, came running towards them.

'Barnes, Barnes!' panted Nigel. 'Please, you've got to come with me. He needs your help again.'

'Who?' asked Friday. Although she suspected she

knew the answer. Nigel had a particularly dim-witted roommate who Friday had assisted before.

'It's Parker,' said Nigel. 'He's in trouble.'

'What's he done this time?' asked Friday.

'He fell asleep on the polo pitch last night,' said Nigel.

'Really?' said Friday. 'I find polo boring, but I don't find it *that* boring.'

'It sounds like the type of thing I would do,' said Melanie.

'That's just it,' said Nigel. 'It doesn't make any sense.'

'Didn't it rain last night?' said Friday. 'There was definitely rumbling of thunder in the distance.'

'It must have rained hard,' said Nigel, 'because Parker was soaked to the skin when they found him.'

'Who found him?' asked Friday.

'The polo team,' said Nigel. 'They have a 6 am practice session.'

'That sounds very early,' said Friday.

'They have to practise harder because Ian has been expelled,' said Melanie. 'He was the best player on the team.'

'So where is Parker now?' asked Friday, ignoring Melanie's reference to Ian.

'He's in sick bay, being treated for hypothermia,' said Nigel.

'I would have thought he'd be happy about that,' said Friday. 'He likes lying around doing nothing.'

'Yes, but he's got an assignment due today,' said Nigel.

'Not with Mr Spencer?' asked Friday.

'It is with Mr Spencer,' said Nigel. 'And you know how much he hates Parker.'

Friday nodded. The answer was a lot. 'But I thought all marks were determined by VP Pete's self-assessment scheme now?' said Friday.

'Mr Spencer did give Parker a chance to do a self-assessment,' said Nigel.

'What happened?' asked Friday.

'He failed himself,' said Nigel.

'Why?' asked Friday.

'Honesty,' said Nigel. 'Parker said he knew better than anyone that he had no idea about chemistry.'

'So not only is Parker seriously ill,' said Friday, 'there's a good chance he will have to repeat chemistry.'

'That would make him seriously ill just to consider,' said Melanie.

'Please, Barnes, you've got to help him,' said Nigel. 'I think Parker has been the victim of some

85

sort of mischief. There must be a reason he was out on the pitch in the pouring rain. I know he's stupid, but he's not *that* stupid.'

'It does sound like a prank gone wrong,' said Friday.

'If you do help,' said Nigel, 'I'm sure Parker will pay you. In fact, *I'll* pay you. I'll let you steal anything you like that belongs to him from our room.'

'Has he got anything I'd want?' asked Friday.

'He's got a lot of Batman comics,' said Nigel.

'Not interested,' said Friday.

'A genuine limited-edition double-ended light sabre,' said Nigel.

'Just because I love science, doesn't mean I'm a nerd,' said Friday.

'At least not that kind of nerd,' said Melanie.

'His aunt sent him a fifty-dollar note,' said Nigel.

'Was it his birthday?' asked Melanie.

'No, it was for growing over 171 centimetres tall,' said Nigel. 'He's the first male in his family to be above average height for three generations.'

'But the average male height is 175 centimetres tall,' said Friday.

'His aunt is eighty-six, so she's still going on 1930s statistics,' said Nigel.

'Fifty dollars will do,' said Friday. 'We'll check it out.'

Sick bay was just along the corridor from the Head-master's office, so none of the secretarial staff batted an eye as Friday walked in with Nigel and Melanie. She was so frequently summoned to the Head-master's office, usually to be yelled at, that they didn't think to question her reason for being there. As the three of them walked down the corridor they could hear yelling, but this time it wasn't the Headmaster.

'It's just not good enough!'

'Isn't that Mr Pilcher's voice?' asked Melanie.

Mr Pilcher was the school groundskeeper. He was a retired army man, and always wore the same tan-coloured work clothes. He prided himself on attending to the school's gardens with military efficiency.

'Yes,' said Friday.

'I wouldn't have thought that someone who works with plants all day could get that angry,' said Melanie.

'The students at this school are a disgrace!' yelled Mr Pilcher.

'It's just a few sweet peas,' said the Headmaster soothingly.

'A few sweet peas?! A FEW SWEET PEAS?!' yelled Mr Pilcher.

'He'll end up in sick bay in a minute,' said Friday. 'From having had an anger-induced stroke.'

'Well, I know who did it,' said Mr Pilcher. 'It's those boys in the medieval re-enactment club. They're always pulling up my canes and pretending they're swords. But goodness knows why they had to go and burn down that dead elm tree on the edge of the swamp!'

'Well, it was dead,' said the Headmaster. 'It will save you having to chop it down.'

'That's not the point!' yelled Mr Pilcher. 'They shouldn't be interfering with my plants, whether they're alive or dead!'

'I'll look into it,' said the Headmaster. 'Would you like a chocolate biscuit?'

This apparently mollified Mr Pilcher because there was no more yelling. Nigel knocked on the door to sick bay and let himself in.

'I've brought someone to see you,' said Nigel.

'Hello,' said Friday.

'Hello, Barnes. Hello, Pelly,' said Parker. 'Are you sick too?'

Parker was lying in bed. He looked pale and tired, but apart from that, much the same as usual.

'No, Nigel was worried about you,' said Friday. 'He's paying me fifty dollars of your money to figure out what happened to you.'

'Apparently I fell asleep in the rain,' said Parker, shifting the pillows so he could sit up a bit more.

'Yes, but that is odd behaviour,' said Friday. 'Is there any reason you might have chosen to do it? Perhaps you couldn't get to sleep and you thought a cold shower of rain might help? Or perhaps you were stargazing, fell asleep and got caught in the rain?'

'Sorry, I just don't know,' said Parker, shaking his head. 'I haven't got the foggiest. I can't remember anything after dinner last night.'

'Do you have a history of sleepwalking?' asked Melanie. 'That's my favourite way to get exercise.'

'I don't think so,' said Parker. He concentrated hard. 'But if I was asleep when I was doing it, I wouldn't be the one to ask, would I? You'd have to ask Nigel.'

'Not that I've noticed,' said Nigel. 'But I'm a sound sleeper.'

'Hmm,' said Friday. 'Do you remember what you were talking about over dinner?'

'Oh, yes,' said Parker, suddenly remembering. 'The curry pie. It was disgusting!'

'I liked it,' said Melanie. 'I thought it was very tasty.'

'Too tasty,' said Parker, with a grimace. 'Mrs Marigold has developed an unnatural obsession with coriander. It's like having toothpaste mixed in with your dinner.'

'Coriander is a very commonly used herb in South East Asian and subcontinent cooking,' said Friday.

'Poor devils,' said Parker. 'You'd think the United Nations would step in and intervene. Show them how to cook a good sausage or something.'

'Aside from the pie, did you have anything on your mind?' asked Friday. 'Anything troubling you?'

'Not at all,' said Parker. 'I'm not one for dwelling on things.'

'You were worried about your history lesson,' Nigel reminded him.

'Oh, yes,' said Parker, frowning as he remembered.

'We've been studying Benjamin Franklin. Painfully dull man. Spent so much of his life worrying about postage stamps. It made it very hard to stay awake.'

'And you were worried about your assignment for Mr Spencer,' added Nigel.

'I was?' said Parker. 'Oh yes, you see that's exactly the type of thing I try to avoid thinking about.'

'So what was your extra credit assignment for Mr Spencer?' asked Friday.

'That's just the problem,' said Parker, throwing up his hands in frustration. 'I could do anything. Anything at all. It's all part of VP Pete's new freedom policies. Now, how am I meant to narrow it down from that? Deciding what to do is harder than the assignment.'

'There must have been some parameters,' said Friday.

'Not really,' said Parker. 'I just had to do an experiment about anything I liked, then write up my method and results. Mr Spencer said I was such a terrible student it was the least challenging assignment he could think of to give me.'

'Interesting,' said Friday. She stood up and walked over to the counter where the school nurse had written up a report on Parker's condition. 'It says here your core body temperature was 35.5 degrees.'

'Yes,' said Parker, pulling the blankets up closer to his chin. 'And I'm not telling you how she measured that. Suffice it to say, I feel violated.'

'Aside from that, you feel well?' asked Friday.

'Fine,' said Parker. 'A bit achy. But I suppose that's to be expected from sleeping on a field in the cold rain.'

Friday continued reading the report. 'The nurse has written that she administered one standard-sized band-aid. Where did she apply it?'

'Oh, that's nothing,' said Parker. 'I had a sore finger. Just a blister.'

'Really?' said Friday. 'May I see?'

'There's nothing to see,' said Parker. 'She put a band-aid over it.' Parker held up his hand to show them. The band-aid had a picture of a pirate on it.

'Nice,' approved Melanie. 'I like a cheerful band-aid.'

'Did you have this blister before you slept on the field?' asked Friday.

'I don't think so,' said Parker, looking at his finger. 'But I did poke my curry pie several times, so it might be a curry burn.'

'Intriguing,' said Friday. 'Nigel, tell me: did anything go missing from your dorm room last night? Other than Parker, of course.'

'No,' said Nigel.

'Are you sure?' asked Friday. 'No lightweight clothing or large sheets of paper?'

'No . . . well, actually, yes!' said Nigel. 'My Spiderman poster went missing from the wall. But I assumed some bully in sixth form took it. They took our sheets and blankets last week, just for a laugh.'

'Parker, do you have your room key?' asked Friday.

'It'd be in my trouser pocket,' said Parker, pointing to where his wet clothes were draped over a chair at the side of the room.

Melanie was closest so she picked up the trousers and checked. 'It's not here.'

'Barnes!'

Friday turned to see the Headmaster standing in the doorway. 'What are you doing here?' he demanded. 'You should be in class.'

'I'm investigating Parker's mysterious accident,' said Friday.

'And admiring his band-aid,' added Melanie.

'There's nothing mysterious about it,' said the Headmaster. 'The fool just took a nap in a rainstorm. He does dim-witted things like that all the time.'

'Actually, Headmaster, you are entirely wrong,' said Friday. 'But before I take you through what really happened, I insist you call an ambulance. Parker should be examined by a cardiologist immediately.'

'But I've just got a sore finger,' protested Parker.

'No, you haven't,' said Friday. 'Well, technically, yes, you have. But in this instance, the small blister on your finger is a symptom of a much more serious incident.'

'It is?' asked Parker.

'You were struck by lightning,' said Friday.

'Preposterous!' said the Headmaster.

'Cool!' said Nigel.

'It is the only explanation that makes sense,' said Friday.

'It doesn't sound sensible at all,' said the Headmaster.

'Parker was given the assignment of conducting an experiment, any experiment,' said Friday. 'He is not a terribly bright or knowledgeable boy.'

'It's true,' agreed Parker, nodding. Melanie patted him on the hand sympathetically.

'He couldn't think of an experiment,' said Friday. 'His understanding of the principles of science is so poor he barely knows what an experiment is.'

'I wanted to ask,' said Parker, 'but I felt silly bringing it up after I'd been studying science for four years.'

'But right before dinner, Parker had been in history class,' said Friday, 'where he had been studying Benjamin Franklin.'

'What, the American politician?' asked the Headmaster.

'Yes, Benjamin Franklin was a politician, as well as a postmaster, a diplomat and a scientist,' said Friday. 'A scientist who performed one of the most famous experiments of all time.'

'Oh dear,' said the Headmaster. 'I think I know where this is going.'

'Benjamin Franklin flew a kite in a rainstorm, using a key as a lightning rod to draw electricity from the clouds into a glass jar,' said Friday.

'I like kites,' said Parker.

'How did you figure all this out?' asked the Headmaster.

'Mr Pilcher is missing some bamboo canes,' said Friday, 'and a poster is missing from Nigel's wall.

They were the clues. When Parker heard the rumble of an electrical storm he had an idea, or, rather, he remembered Benjamin Franklin's idea. Parker didn't have a kite, so he made one with the canes and the poster and rushed out into the rain. He tied his room key to the string, launched the kite and tested his hypothesis. And like almost everyone who has attempted this experiment other than Benjamin Franklin, Parker was struck by lightning.'

'And that's why my finger hurts?' asked Parker.

'It's the entrance wound,' explained Friday. 'The electrical surge would have streamed down the wet string to the hand you were holding it with, then passed through your body into the wet ground. That's why your muscles are achy. Your entire body spent three milliseconds in total spasm.'

'My goodness!' exclaimed the Headmaster. He leant out into the corridor and called to his receptionist. 'Miss Pritchard, call an ambulance – now!' He turned back, in to the room. 'Just think of the lawsuits.'

'It's not so bad,' said Friday. 'Several people have died trying to copy this experiment.'

'But what about my assignment?' said Parker. 'What will Mr Spencer say?'

'He can't complain,' said Melanie. 'You did conduct an experiment.'

'And you certainly had dramatic results,' added Friday.

'But I'm going to have to write it all up,' said Parker. 'And my finger hurts.'

'Just hand in a charred branch from the burnt elm tree on the edge of the forest,' suggested Friday.

'What's that got to do with anything?' asked Parker.

'When your kite was struck by lightning, it would have caught fire,' explained Friday. 'Then when you lost consciousness, it would have blown away until it caught on the tree. It's an excellent example of cause and effect. If you write it up, even Mr Spencer will have to pass you.'

Chapter 11

In Trouble Again

Two days later, Friday and Melanie were sitting through a particularly ridiculous English lesson. Mrs Cannon never followed a conventional syllabus. She preferred going through the job ads and doing the crossword with her class. But things had become even more extreme. VP Pete had decided to take over her lessons for a week, and the situation had quickly degenerated into farce.

All the chairs and desks had been removed. VP Pete stood in the doorway while the class filed in.

'Where are we supposed to sit?' asked Friday.

'Anywhere on the floor,' said VP Pete. 'I want to challenge the assumptions of traditional education. I don't want conforming to standard furniture to affect the way you appreciate literature.'

'I don't think it was the furniture that was holding us back,' said Melanie. 'I think it had more to do with the painfully boring novels on the curriculum.'

'Are the novels boring?' asked VP Pete. 'Or was the way you were taught about them boring?'

'It was definitely the novels,' said Rajiv.

'Yes, well, I'm here to deconstruct the educational norm,' said VP Pete, producing a big bag of toilet paper. 'I want you all to sit in a circle. I'm going to hand around a roll of toilet paper and I want you each to take some.'

'You aren't going to make us do something disgusting, are you?' asked Mirabella.

'No, not unless you want to,' said VP Pete, handing her a roll. 'In which case, I will not project my values onto your actions to label them in any way.'

The toilet paper made it around the room until everyone had a wad in their hand.

'Now,' said VP Pete as he sat down in the circle,

'we are going to play a game. You have to tell the group a secret about yourself for each square of paper you have in your hand.'

The people who had taken large wads of paper groaned.

'I'll go first,' said VP Pete. 'My name is VP Pete and my secret is that I have an irresistible urge to eat cake. I just love it.'

Friday snorted.

'Is there something you want to say, Miss Barnes?' asked VP Pete.

'It's not much of a secret, is it?' said Friday.

'Friday,' warned Melanie. 'Careful.'

'No, this is a safe environment,' said VP Pete with a smile. 'Say what you want to say.'

'For a start, everyone likes cake,' said Friday. 'It's like saying you like sunsets or rainbows. Then, obviously, you specifically really like cake because . . .' Friday gestured towards VP Pete and then in a flash of insight realised she should not say what she was about to say so she fell silent.

'Because what?' asked VP Pete. He was still smiling with his mouth, but his eyes had narrowed.

'I have nothing further to say on this subject,' said Friday.

'Really?' said VP Pete, tilting his head to one side. 'I know you like observing things, so you didn't want to observe that I was fat?'

Friday shook her head and stared at the floor. She wanted to scream 'Of course you're fat! You must be at least twenty-five kilos over the healthy weight range!' but she knew this would be considered impolite.

'All right,' said VP Pete. 'Let's move on. Who wants to go first?'

Now everyone was staring at the floor.

'Peregrine,' snapped VP Pete. 'You start us off. Tell us a secret about yourself.'

Peregrine looked terrified. 'Do I have to, sir?'

'Don't call me "sir". This school does not subscribe to those hierarchical titles anymore,' said VP Pete. 'You must call me VP Pete. You are to call all your teachers by their first names. It's for your own good. Now, tell us a secret about yourself. This is a safe environment, so no one will judge you here.'

'Yes, si– Pete. Um . . .' began Peregrine. 'Once I was at the mini-market in town and I didn't have any money, so I shoplifted a Milky Way bar.'

VP Pete leapt to his feet. 'You stole! You despicable boy! Go to the Headmaster's office at once! This has to be reported to the police.'

'But you said this was a safe environment!' protested Friday.

'Not for criminals!' declared VP Pete, pointing at the doorway. 'Get out of my sight, boy!'

Peregrine got to his feet and ran, but when he got to the doorway he slammed into another boy trying to come in. They both fell over.

'What do you want?!' yelled VP Pete at the hapless new arrival.

'There's a phone call,' said the boy.

'I can't take it, I'm teaching a class,' snapped VP Pete.

'Not for you, sir,' said the boy. 'It's for Friday. An urgent matter.'

'She can't take it, she's in a class,' yelled VP Pete.

'If I told you that I'd done lots of shoplifting as well, would you let me go and take the call?' asked Friday.

'Just get out!' yelled VP Pete. 'But you have to write me a 10,000 word self-analysis and have it on my desk by first thing tomorrow.'

'Fine,' said Friday as she left, taking a shell-shocked Peregrine with her.

When Friday picked up the phone in the school office she recognised the heavy breathing on the other end. 'Uncle Bernie?'

'Friday, thank goodness! You've got to come at once,' said Uncle Bernie.

'Are you in the bathroom?' asked Friday.

'What?' asked Uncle Bernie.

'Your voice sounds echoey, as if you're talking to me on your phone from inside a bathroom,' said Friday.

'So?' asked Uncle Bernie.

'I refuse to talk to you,' said Friday. 'It's un-hygienic.'

'I just stepped into the bathroom to get some privacy,' said Uncle Bernie. 'Helena is in a state.'

'Who's Helena?' asked Friday.

'Helena Wainscott,' said Uncle Bernie.

'Ian's mum?' said Friday.

'Yes,' said Uncle Bernie. 'She's very upset.'

'Exactly what is the nature of your relationship with Mrs Wainscott?' asked Friday.

'That's none of your business,' said Uncle Bernie.

'I thought as much,' said Friday. 'The juicy details never are.'

'We're not talking about her,' said Uncle Bernie.

'You're the one who brought up her name,' said Friday.

'Well, yes, we are talking about her,' said Uncle Bernie, 'but not about her and me.'

'So there is a "her and you", you admit it!' said Friday.

'I'm the one who taught you how to cross-examine people,' said Uncle Bernie. 'You can't use those tricks on me.'

'Too late, I already did,' said Friday. 'So what does your girlfriend need help with now?'

'Ian is going to be expelled,' said Uncle Bernie.

'You're behind the times,' said Friday. 'He was expelled three weeks ago.'

'No, from his new school,' said Uncle Bernie. 'And let me tell you, it takes quite something to get expelled from this school.'

'What did he do?' asked Friday.

'He was caught stealing exam papers,' said Uncle Bernie.

'Okay, that doesn't sound right. You need to get out of that bathroom and come and get me right away,' said Friday. 'As soon as you've washed your hands, that is.'

Two hours later, Uncle Bernie picked up Friday and Melanie from the front of the school. Friday had told the Headmaster that her uncle was having a medical crisis and she needed to go right away because she was his nearest bone marrow match. The Headmaster did not believe her, but he asked Friday not to tell him any more details in case he should be called upon to give evidence in court. He shooed her and Melanie away as quickly as possible.

'We've got a ninety-minute drive to Ian's school,' said Friday, as she slid into the beaten-up old sedan. 'Fill us in on all the details.'

'Yes,' agreed Melanie. 'Are you and Mrs Wainscott going to get married? If so, will Friday be a brides-maid? And will that make Ian her cousin?! Ew, gross!'

'I meant the details of the case against Ian,' said Friday.

'Oh yes, let's talk about that,' said Melanie. 'It's less disturbing.'

'He was caught in the headmaster's office, with the filing cabinet open, taking the exam papers out,' said Uncle Bernie.

'What were the exams for?' asked Friday.

'It was a maths exam,' said Uncle Bernie.

'But Ian is excellent at maths,' said Friday. 'Considering how little access he has had to university-level academic research, it's impressive that his understanding of mathematics is almost as good as mine.'

'Maybe he's fallen in with a bad crowd?' said Melanie.

'As opposed to all the wonderful influences at Highcrest?' said Friday ironically.

'Actually, the opposite is true,' said Uncle Bernie. 'He's been tutoring the other students.'

'How noble,' said Melanie.

'For money,' added Uncle Bernie.

'And pragmatic,' said Melanie.

'The school's saying that's why these kids have

been doing so well, because he's been stealing the weekly pop quizzes,' said Uncle Bernie.

'He is good at stealing things,' said Friday, lost in thought.

'Please don't say that when we get there,' said Uncle Bernie. 'His mum is going to be ever so upset if we land him in even more trouble.'

Chapter 12

Ian's New School

When Uncle Bernie pulled up outside Ian's new school, Melanie had fallen asleep during the car ride. Friday looked about at the school buildings and was pleasantly surprised. It looked very nice. The administration block was a brand new building and through a gaudy use of primary colours it looked quite cheerful.

'This school looks nice,' said Friday. 'I was expecting it to be old and rundown.'

'Yes,' said Uncle Bernie. 'A year nine boy burned the main building down two years ago. So this new building has only been in use for a couple of months.'

'What's the library like?' asked Friday as she followed her uncle into the school office. They left Melanie asleep in the car, with a window open and a note pinned to her chest explaining where she was.

'Excellent,' said Uncle Bernie. 'The entire collection was ruined last year in a flood, so the school was able to buy all new books with the insurance money.'

'It sounds like they must have very high insurance premiums,' said Friday.

'Oh yes,' said Uncle Bernie. He was an insurance investigator, so he was an expert on such matters. 'You should have seen the claim they made for their rat problem.'

'Rat problem?!' said Friday.

'It's under control now,' said Uncle Bernie. 'For the most part.'

Once Uncle Bernie and Friday had signed in, the receptionist led them through a glass door towards the principal's office. There was a bench outside and a scruffy boy wearing the all-grey school uniform was slumped on it. It was only when Friday was a metre away that she realised who it was.

'Ian!' exclaimed Friday.

Ian looked up and sneered. 'What are you doing here? Ruining the lives of everyone at one school not enough for you anymore?'

Friday wasn't listening. She couldn't get over the way Ian looked. If she had not known objectively that he was extremely handsome, she could easily not have noticed today. The ugly school uniform seemed to suck the colour from his face and the spirit from his demeanour.

'I'm here to get you out of trouble,' said Friday.

'Why can't you mind your own business?' asked Ian.

'Your mother is upset,' said Friday.

'Upset that if I'm at home more I'll distract her from her winter pruning,' said Ian. Mrs Wainscott was a keen vegetable gardener.

'Is that self-pity I hear from the great Ian Wainscott?' asked Friday.

Ian straightened up on the bench and pushed his fringe out of his eyes. 'When I need help – which I don't – I'll ask for it, which I'm not.'

'You're not my client,' said Friday. 'Your mother is.'

The principal's door opened and a flurry of batik rushed at Friday.

'Thank goodness you're here!' said Mrs Wainscott as she enveloped Friday in a huge hug. 'Don't let them kick my boy out!'

'We're not kicking anyone anywhere,' said a very reasonable-looking middle-aged woman standing behind her. 'Hello, I'm Mrs Hurst. We don't expel students for this type of thing. But stealing exam papers is very serious. There is a mandatory punishment of two weeks suspension.'

'Hello, Mrs Hurst,' said Uncle Bernie. 'I'm Bernard Barnes.'

Ian sniggered. 'Bernard.'

'This is my niece, Friday,' continued Uncle Bernie. 'She's a friend of Ian's . . .'

Ian interrupted with a scoffing noise.

'Well, she knows Ian from his old school,' said Uncle Bernie. 'And –'

Mrs Wainscott interrupted at this point. 'She is a brilliant investigative detective and she's going to see to it that my boy is not wrongly convicted of a crime he didn't commit!'

Now, you have to understand, Mrs Hurst was the headmistress of a very challenging school, and having a twelve-year-old girl turn up claiming to be a detective was nowhere near the top ten of bizarre things she had to deal with in a given week. In her line of work, Mrs Hurst had learned to take the path of least resistance where possible, so when confronted with a scruffy girl in a brown cardigan planning to overturn her disciplinary decision, she simply smiled, nodded, and said, 'I see.'

'If the punishment is two weeks suspension,' said Friday, turning to Uncle Bernie, 'are you sure that Ian didn't commit the crime just to get a holiday?'

'Thanks,' said Ian. 'It's nice to know you have such a high regard for my character.'

'You've got to investigate,' said Mrs Wainscott. 'Show them that just because his father is a convicted criminal and he's been thrown out of one school for large-scale forgery, Ian isn't really a bad boy.'

'You can see why she gave away her career as a defence lawyer,' said Ian, rolling his eyes. (Mrs Wainscott literally had been a defence lawyer at one time, but she had thrown it in to pursue a career in the circus, which is where she met Ian's dad.)

'I'd like to inspect the scene of the crime,' said Friday.

'Friday, "alleged". Can't you say "alleged"?' urged Uncle Bernie.

'There's no "alleged" about it,' said Friday. 'Either Ian stole the paper or he has been falsely accused of stealing the paper. Either way, a crime has taken place.'

'You're welcome to come and have a look,' said the Mrs Hurst kindly. 'There's not much to see.'

'Thank you,' said Friday before turning to Uncle Bernie and giving him a meaningful glare. 'Perhaps you and Mrs Wainscott should stay out here.' She waggled her eyebrows at her uncle hoping he would get the hint.

Uncle Bernie immediately understood: Mrs Wainscott's hysterics might hinder the investigation. 'Come on, Helena, let's find you a cup of organic chai. Friday will sort this out. You've had quite a shock.' He led Mrs Wainscott away.

Ian rolled his eyes. 'She had quite a shock in that she might have to spend time with me if I was home from school for two weeks.'

Friday and Ian followed Mrs Hurst into her office. Mrs Hurst was right. There wasn't much to see.

A large office desk was covered in paperwork and stationery. Venetian blinds with a broken cord shaded the window. Three four-drawer filing cabinets were stacked side by side in the corner of the room. On the wall hung a framed photograph of the entire student body. And a golf umbrella sat in the corner, although Friday doubted anyone at the school played golf.

Friday closely inspected the photograph. Ian wasn't in it. It must have been taken earlier in the year.

'So what happened?' asked Friday.

'I had been called out into the playground,' said Mrs Hurst. 'One of the younger students had an upset stomach.'

'Animesh had thrown up all over the basketball court,' said Ian.

'Yes, it only took a minute to deal with that. Mr Burgess, the janitor, soon brought out the high-pressure hose and took care of it,' said Mrs Hurst. 'When I got back to the office, I found Ian taking the papers out of the filing cabinet.'

'Really?' said Friday, going over to the filing cabinets herself. She closely inspected each cabinet, the floor in front of them and the wall above.

The floor was covered in cheap synthetic carpet, already worn from hard use. Crumpled-up gum wrappers were wedged down the side of the filing cabinets. The wall behind was white and showed every stain. Water was leaking from the air conditioning vent directly above. Further down the wall, was a black smudge like someone had dragged a squash ball down the paintwork. There was a clutter of paperwork on top of the cabinets.

Friday carefully moved the paperwork to one side, but there wasn't much to see underneath, just a dent where something heavy had been dropped on the metal surface. 'Which drawer held the exams?'

'The second drawer down in the third cabinet away from the window,' said Mrs Hurst.

Friday rolled out the drawer. It contained dozens of hanging files. 'What was the paper filed under? "M" for maths? "P" for pop quiz? "E" for exam paper?'

'No it was filed under W for WMSA,' said Mrs Hurst.

'Wmsa?' asked Friday.

'Weekly Mathematics Skills Assessment,' said Mrs Hurst.

Friday flicked through the hanging files until she found the one marked WMSA. 'And how did Ian get into the office?' asked Friday.

'He walked in,' said Mrs Hurst. 'He'd told the receptionist he needed to leave something on my desk. The receptionist has only been working here for three days, and she hasn't worked with children before. It didn't occur to her to stop him.'

'Sorry, Ian,' said Friday. 'You're not going to get that two-week holiday.'

'Rats,' said Ian.

'Exactly,' said Friday. 'Rats.'

'Rats stole the paper?' asked Mrs Hurst.

'No, but they inadvertently contributed to the crime,' said Friday.

'What's she talking about?' asked Mrs Hurst, turning to Ian.

'I don't know,' said Ian. 'But she'll tell us eventually once we're all so irritated that we want to kill her.'

'Clearly, the paper was stolen,' said Friday.

'I thought you were meant to be getting me off,' said Ian.

'But not by Ian,' said Friday. 'You've had pest controllers in here dealing with a rat problem. To deal with rats, pest controllers lay bait stations around the gardens and in the air conditioning vents.' She pointed to the vent above the filing cabinets. 'Pest controllers earn approximately twenty-two dollars an hour – which isn't much, considering they spend their whole day crawling about in dark, confined spaces full of rat poo and spiders. As a result, they tend to be bitter and resentful, so they are prone to cutting corners. Such as not screwing the vent outlet covers back on properly.'

Friday picked up Mrs Hurst's golf umbrella and flicked the corner of the air conditioning vent. The cover fell off and dropped to the top of the filing cabinet. 'Thus providing an access point for the wily thief.'

'What are you talking about?' said Mrs Hurst. 'Ian just walked right in. All the office staff saw him.'

'Yes, they saw him,' said Friday, 'but he wasn't the thief. The real thief climbed down into your office from the air conditioning vent. You'll notice the black scuff mark on the wall. That's consistent with someone who is approximately five-foot-four tall hanging out of the vent by their waist and scrambling to find purchase with their feet. Then they simply dropped down, causing this dent in the top of the filing cabinet.'

'Anything could have caused that,' said Mrs Hurst, peering at the black mark.

'But did it?' said Friday. 'Had you noticed this dent before?'

'No,' conceded Mrs Hurst, running her finger along the indentation. 'But all the furniture around here is so dented, I might have just not noticed.'

'Then the thief had to get down to the floor,' said Friday. 'These cabinets are 1.2 metres high. That's too far to jump, so they tried to lower themselves to the ground using the cord from the Venetian blind, which is why it is broken.'

'I assumed the cleaning staff did that,' said Mrs Hurst, picking up the broken cord.

Friday shook her head. 'People always blame the cleaning staff,' she said sadly. 'Then the thief found the paper, which would have taken a while because there are twelve drawers here to search through. They chewed three pieces of Juicy Loosy gum while they searched, and shoved the wrappers down the side of the cabinet. They found the test papers, climbed back up onto the filing cabinet, leaving a partial shoe print on the corner of the windowsill, then up into the air conditioning vent. I can see the grubby fingerprints from here – it looks like they had Cheezels for lunch. Then they pulled the vent cover back into place behind them before making good their escape.'

'But I caught Ian taking the paper,' said Mrs Hurst.

'No, you caught him in your office with the drawer open and the paper in his hand,' said Friday. 'But he wasn't taking it. He was returning it.'

'That's impossible to prove,' said Mrs Hurst, shaking her head.

'Not at all,' said Friday. 'You were gone for less than a minute because the janitor quickly brought out his high-pressure hose. So, if you subtract the time it took Ian to walk into the building, speak to the receptionist and get into your office, he only had about thirty seconds before you found him.'

'That would have been plenty of time to steal the exam papers,' said Mrs Hurst.

'No it wouldn't,' said Friday. 'You have a shamefully illogical filing system. There is an entire wall of files here. There is no way Ian could have found the right hanging file that quickly unless he already had the paper in his hand and he could see the ridiculous acronym WMSA written on the top.'

'But if Ian didn't take it, who did?' said Mrs Hurst.

'Do we have to go through this?' asked Ian. 'I'm happy to take the rap. The paper has been returned. No harm, no foul.'

'I want to know who broke into my office,' said Mrs Hurst sternly. 'Maybe it was Ian, and he felt guilty so he returned the paper himself?'

'No,' said Friday. 'Ian's shoulders are too broad to fit into the air conditioning vent.'

'You're obsessed with my body, aren't you?' said Ian.

'Your thief is five-foot-four tall, slim, chews Juicy Loosy gum, is poor at maths, likes Cheezels, has wiry strength but not a lot of common sense, and is someone Ian would want to protect,' said Friday. 'Do any of his tutoring students meet that description?'

'You don't care whose life you screw up, do you?' accused Ian.

'Cheating in exams is a serious crime,' declared Friday, turning to Ian.

'No, it's not,' said Ian. 'It's the very definition of unserious.'

'That isn't even a proper word,' said Friday.

'Unserious unserious unserious,' said Ian.

'But cheating devalues the whole examination system,' said Friday. 'It makes comparative analysis useless.'

'Which doesn't matter because comparative analysis is *unserious*,' said Ian.

'I asked for all of Ian's tutoring buddies to be brought to my office,' said Mrs Hurst. 'They should be waiting outside.'

Friday went straight to the door and stepped out into the corridor.

There were three students sitting on the bench. One was a really tall and athletic boy who looked like he played a lot of some sort of football, or was in training to be a professional wrestler. Then there was a thin boy whose leg was in a cast from toe to hip. From the amount of misspelled messages scrawled on his cast, it had clearly been there for some time. The third student was a short, wiry girl who was chewing gum and listening to music through earbuds.

'Stephanie Gerraldi,' said Mrs Hurst with an exasperated sigh.

Stephanie didn't even look up. The music in her earbuds was so loud her head just bopped along.

'Don't punish her,' urged Ian. 'She didn't actually cheat. When she showed me the paper, I told her off and took them to put back. She just wanted to do well in her exam.'

'She broke into my office,' said Mrs Hurst.

'To be fair,' said Friday, 'the way she broke in took impressive athleticism and ingenuity. You could give her an extra credit for PE, at the very least. But if you could train her to transfer that non-linear thinking and three-dimensional problem solving into mathematics, she could be a geometry genius.'

'If I thought that she was going to take her success here as encouragement to pursue maths, I might,' said Mrs Hurst. 'But I know Stephanie. She's more likely to take it as encouragement to pursue housebreaking. I have to suspend her.'

'Thanks, Friday,' said Ian. 'Yet again, you've been technically right, but totally failed at being a decent human being.'

'Might I suggest,' said Friday, 'that instead of suspending her, you send Stephanie to the University to do a two-week internship. I know a professor of geometry who would love to have an assistant for a fortnight, and he loves explaining mathematical concepts to people whether they want to hear them or not.'

'Do you think she'd go for it?' asked Mrs Hurst, looking at Stephanie chewing gum and moving to the music from her earbuds.

'If Stephanie is lazy and prefers to take shortcuts,' said Friday, 'then the academic life could be perfect for her.'

Ian slouched off across the playground, just calling 'See you at home' over his shoulder to his mother.

'He really misses Highcrest,' said Mrs Wainscott. 'He isn't himself. It's like there's not enough scope for his imagination here.'

'He just doesn't like regular school because six hours a day isn't enough for him to cook up his wicked plans,' said Friday. 'Hey Ian, wait up!'

Friday jogged over to catch up with Ian. He stopped to wait for her but didn't turn around.

'I just wanted to say goodbye,' said Friday. 'We're going.'

'Whatever.' Ian shrugged.

Friday reached out and touched him on the arm. 'Hey, are you all right?'

Ian looked at her. 'You can't solve everyone's problems. You're not Superman.'

'No,' agreed Friday. 'I might have no fashion

sense, but even I know not to wear underpants on the outside.'

'But you forget to zip up,' said Ian.

Friday looked down at her jeans.

'Made you look,' said Ian.

'Are you okay here?' asked Friday.

'I'm fine,' said Ian. 'King of the school.' He smiled his smarmy smile. The effect was immediately ruined by a football slamming into the side of his head.

'Whoops, sorry, newbie,' called a large athletic boy from the other side of the playground. His friends sniggered.

'King of the school, huh?' said Friday.

'I've only been here three weeks,' said Ian. 'It's going to take a while to let everyone else know it.' He stalked away.

Chapter 13

Something in the Stroganoff

Two weeks later Friday and Melanie were still getting used to the new free-form curriculum. As part of their general studies class, they had been told to teach themselves an important life skill. So Melanie had taught herself how to get dressed without getting out of bed, an invaluable skill on a cold winter's morning. And Friday had been trying to teach herself how to pick the lock on a pair of handcuffs with a paperclip.

Friday had handcuffed herself to the leg of her desk and spent two hours twiddling with the tumblers one at a time to no avail. She finally gave up when the clock ticked over to 6 o'clock, the time when dinner was served. It was beef stroganoff night. This was a new addition to the weekly menu, and Mrs Marigold believed in using hearty quantities of full fat cream, so it was delicious. Friday's need to escape had become serious.

When she had first cuffed herself to the furniture, Friday had given Melanie the key to hold. Unfortunately, Melanie had become so bored in the first five minutes that she predictably fell into slumber. At the two-hour mark, she was in the deepest depths of REM sleep. No amount of loud yelling could wake her. And Friday didn't have her arms free so she couldn't throw desktop objects at her friend or pour a glass of water over her, as she normally would. Friday spent twenty minutes trying to build a mini catapult out of her stapler and a packet of thumbtacks. But the projectile couldn't reach Melanie, who was four metres away on the bed.

In the end Friday gave up, and desperately resumed her attempts to pick the handcuff lock. This time, the lock popped in less than four minutes. It's amazing the motivating power a bowl of hot beef stewed in sour cream can have.

As Friday and Melanie walked into the dining room half an hour after the dinner service had begun, the dining hall was already full. The room smelled heavenly. The scent of beef, mushrooms and cream, served on a bed of rice was divine. Beef stroganoff was the perfect comfort food after a long, cold winter's day being mentally assaulted by the educational intentions of the teaching staff.

'I'm so hungry,' said Friday. 'I thought I was hungry before, but now that I can actually smell food, I'm starving.'

'I'm hungry too,' said Melanie with a yawn. 'Napping always works up my appetite.'

They picked up a tray each and joined the back of the queue.

'I hope Mrs Marigold has made her crusty bread rolls,' said Friday. 'I want to be able to soak up all the sauce.'

'It's awfully quiet today,' said Melanie.

Friday looked around at the dining hall. Considering that the large room was entirely full of students it was unusually quiet. Very little conversation was taking place.

'The food must be so good they're all focusing on eating,' said Friday, sliding her tray forward and handing her plate to Mrs Marigold, who dished up a generous portion of rice, then ladled a huge steaming serving of stroganoff on top, the thick gravy pooling on the plate and soaking into the rice.

'Yum,' said Friday.

'Bleurrggh!'

The horrible guttural noise could mean only one thing. Friday turned around to see that Jessica Bastionne had been sick all over the floor.

'I've lost my appetite,' said Melanie.

'I'm going to be sick too!' declared Trea Babcock as she leapt to her feet and ran for the bathroom.

Now several people started moaning.

'Bllaaaggrh!'

Peregrine had been sick in a potted plant.

'This is not good,' said Friday.

'What's happening?' asked Mrs Marigold.

'You'd better call the Headmaster,' said Friday. 'It looks like the entire school is coming down with food poisoning.'

Chapter 14

A Conspiracy

By the time the Headmaster arrived, the dining hall was in utter chaos. Friday had taken charge and set up a triage system. Anyone who actually threw up was sent to sick bay, where the school nurse had ample buckets on hand and rehydration formula at the ready. Anyone who felt like they were going to be sick was sent to lie on the floor by the windows.

The long tables had been dragged to the side of the room and stacked up to make space. The tall sash windows had been thrown open, despite the cold of the night, to let in fresh air and let out the horrible smell.

Mr Pilcher was doing sterling work. He whisked the hapless potted plant outside and cleaned up Jessica and Peregrine's mess in quick time. So now the dining hall was simply a room full of students lying on the ground, clutching their stomachs and moaning.

'What on earth is going on here?' demanded the Headmaster as he burst in and saw 75 per cent of the student body lying ill on the floor.

'Everyone's sick,' said Friday.

'I can see that!' said the Headmaster. 'Sick with what?'

'It looks like food poisoning,' said Friday.

'How dare you!' yelled Mrs Marigold. 'I'll have you know I only use the finest ingredients. I have been cooking for forty years and I have never given anyone food poisoning.'

'What about the Indonesian ambassador?' asked Melanie.

Mrs Marigold went bright red and quivered with fury. 'That was "poison" poisoning – there is a difference!' She looked like she was about to burst into tears.

'We've got no time for recriminations,' said the Headmaster. 'We need to get to the bottom of this urgently before the students get any sicker.'

'It has to be the beef stroganoff,' said Friday.

Mrs Marigold gasped. 'But you said it was sublime when I served it last week.' There were definitely tears running down the cook's face now.

'But look,' said Friday, indicating the twenty or so students who were standing about, still in good health, 'the vegetarians are all right.'

'All those students are vegetarians?' asked the Headmaster. 'I didn't realise we had so many of them.'

'Low carb, low protein diets are very fashionable right now,' explained Melanie.

'I'm not a vegetarian,' protested Lizzie Abercrombie petulantly. 'Max and I are lactose intolerant. We can't eat beef stroganoff because of the cream.'

'It makes us fart,' said Max.

'Max!' exclaimed Lizzie.

'It's true!' protested Max. 'One glass of milk and Lizzie sounds like a whoopee cushion – *prrbt, prrbt.*'

'Shut up, Max!' yelled Lizzie.

'Silence!' ordered the Headmaster. 'With three-quarters of the student body poisoned, now is not the time to indulge in scatological humour.'

'*Prrbt,*' concluded Max.

'Well, Melanie and I are fine,' said Friday, 'because we didn't eat anything at all. So it must be the beef stroganoff.'

'I'm glad I had a tin of baked beans in my study,' said the Headmaster.

'I knew it!' accused Mrs Marigold, wagging her finger at the Headmaster. 'I knew you had been secretly cooking for yourself.'

'It's not your cooking I'm avoiding,' said the Headmaster. 'It's the dinner table conversation with the other teachers. I can never make it to the dessert course without one of them asking for a raise.'

'So what was in your stroganoff?' asked Friday.

'Beef, obviously,' said Mrs Marigold. 'Sour cream . . .'

'How sour?' asked the Headmaster.

'It's not regular cream gone sour,' said Mrs Marigold. 'It's sour cream from the supermarket. I bought it this morning. Its use-by date isn't for another month.'

'What else is in the dinner?' asked Friday.

'Just mushrooms,' said Mrs Marigold.

'Mushrooms?' said Friday, her ears pricking up. 'Where did you get the mushrooms from?'

'I use a variety,' said Mrs Marigold. 'I get regular mushrooms from the supermarket, shiitake mushrooms from the greengrocer, and Mr Pilcher picked some mushrooms for me down in the forest.'

They all swivelled round to look at Mr Pilcher. He was dutifully mopping the floor with disinfectant.

Friday was fond of Mr Pilcher. He had been very grateful to her for catching the student who hit him over the back of the head with a shovel just the previous term. And she was very grateful that he had let her borrow gardening tools without asking too many questions. Friday knew the line of questioning she was about to engage in was sure to stretch their friendship.

'Mr Pilcher,' Friday began politely, 'Mrs Marigold says you picked some mushrooms for her down in the forest.'

'Yes, that's right,' said Mr Pilcher. 'With the rain yesterday, there was a good big crop of them.'

'Do you remember what sort of tree you found them under?' asked Friday.

'I don't know,' said Mr Pilcher. 'An oak, I suppose. There was a clump of oak trees in that part of the forest.'

'Oh dear,' said Friday.

'What?!' demanded the Headmaster. 'What is it?'

Friday held up her hand to silence him for a moment.

'Mr Pilcher, what colour were the mushrooms?' asked Friday.

'White, mainly,' said Mr Pilcher.

'Plain white?' asked Friday.

'Well, you know how mushrooms are in the wild. Off-white, I'd say,' said Mr Pilcher.

'Excuse me,' said Lizzie Abercrombie as she approached the group.

'What is it, girl?' asked the Headmaster.

'It's just, I saw Mr Pilcher picking the mushrooms under the oak tree,' said Lizzie. 'If the colour is important, I distinctly saw that they had a green tinge.'

Mr Maclean, the geography teacher, pushed his way through the crowd.

'This is serious,' said Mr Maclean. 'Someone call an ambulance. Call a fleet of ambulances!'

'What's going on?!' demanded the Headmaster.

'A white mushroom with a green tinge that grows under an oak tree,' said Mr Maclean, 'is the deathcap!'

Everyone who was well enough to be paying attention gasped.

'The deathcap,' continued Mr Maclean, 'is the most dangerous fungus in the world. If these students have all eaten deathcap mushrooms, they're going to die!'

'Good heavens,' said the Headmaster.

'Wait!' said Friday.

'There's no time to wait,' said Mr Maclean. 'We've got to get the students to hospital. They need to have their stomachs pumped. They need to be on IVs. They need to be on the waiting list for liver transplants. This is deadly serious.'

'No!' said Friday.

'What do you mean "no"?!' said the Headmaster. 'Three-quarters of the student body has been poisoned – it doesn't get more serious than that! This will be the end of Highcrest. It will be the end of me.'

'No one has been poisoned,' said Friday. 'Well, obviously, everyone has been poisoned. But not by deathcap mushrooms.'

'How can you possibly know that?' asked the Headmaster.

'You like to make out that you know everything, Barnes,' said Mr Maclean, 'but in this instance I know more. My master's degree is in forest fungi. I recognise the description of a deathcap when I hear one.'

'How does a degree in fungus qualify Mr Maclean to be a geography teacher?' asked Melanie.

'Fungi live in forests, forests are an ecosystem, ecosystems are something you study in geography,' said Friday.

'Talk about six degrees of separation,' said Melanie.

'These children are dying of mushroom poisoning!' wailed Mr Maclean. 'This will be the end of Highcrest Academy!'

'These students can't have eaten a deathcap,' said Friday, 'because they are too sick.'

'What?' asked the Headmaster.

'If you eat a deathcap mushroom,' said Friday, 'it takes two to three hours for symptoms of nausea to occur. These students started throwing up after twenty minutes.'

'Maybe it's a new strain of deathcap,' said Mr Maclean. 'One with even *stronger* poison.'

'Or maybe it's something else entirely,' said

Friday. 'Mrs Marigold, I'd like to inspect the scene of the crime.'

'What?' said Mrs Marigold. 'I haven't committed a crime.'

'You haven't,' said Friday. 'But someone has.'

Friday made her way into the kitchen. On the stove was a huge pot. It was three-quarters empty. But at the bottom sat three inches of bubbling hot beef stroganoff.

Mr Maclean covered his face with his tie.

'Don't go near it,' said Mr Maclean. 'The fumes could be deadly. Headmaster, you need to call in a hazmat team.'

Friday ignored Mr Maclean. She picked up a wooden spoon and tentatively gave the beef mixture a stir. 'There's a lot of stew left over,' observed Friday.

'I was going to use the leftovers to make pie for the weekend,' said Mrs Marigold.

'I like pie,' said Melanie.

'Everyone likes pie,' said Mrs Marigold, breaking down into tears. 'It's because my pastry is so light and fluffy.' She degenerated into wracking sobs, pulling up the hem of her apron to dab the corners of her eyes.

Friday carefully stirred the stew in small circles.

'What are you doing?' asked the Headmaster.

'Searching,' said Friday.

'For mushrooms?' asked the Headmaster.

'No,' said Friday. Her spoon knocked something solid against the side of the pot. 'Aha!'

'What is it?' said Melanie.

'Let's see,' said Friday. She carefully scooped out a small glass jar. It was covered in brown creamy sauce. Friday used the spoon to carry it over to the sink, turned on the tap and rinsed the sauce away. 'Just as I suspected.'

'What?' asked the Headmaster.

Friday picked up the bottle in her hand. 'Ipecac syrup,' said Friday. 'It's considered old-fashioned now, but ipecac syrup is actually a treatment for poisoning. If you take it, it makes you throw up. Doctors used to use it to get poison out of a patient's stomach.'

'So it's harmless?' said the Headmaster.

'No, it'll make you throw up,' said Friday. 'But that's all. It won't cause liver failure, kidney failure and cardiac arrest like a deathcap would.'

'But who would put a bottle of ipecac in my beef stroganoff?' said Mrs Marigold. She was pulling herself together now, thanks to the recuperative power of anger.

'More importantly,' said Friday, 'who would want to make it look like the whole school had been poisoned by deadly mushrooms?'

'It's the type of thing Ian might do,' said Melanie.

'What?!' exploded the Headmaster. 'That boy's expelled. He's at some state school two hours' drive away.' He slumped down on a chair. 'Oh no, you don't think he's masterminded the whole thing from a distance, do you? He's probably trying to destabilise the school so it will be closed down as an act of revenge. That's just what I need – a vengeful ex-student causing chaos.'

'No, of course not,' said Friday. 'I'm sure Ian is playing elaborate pranks on his own school now. There's bound to be someone else with a motive to cause mayhem here.'

'The vegetarians?' said Melanie.

'They don't have enough energy to cause trouble,' said Mrs Marigold. 'They don't get enough protein. The human body was not designed to be fuelled by chickpeas.'

'But they are the only ones who weren't endangered by the ipecac syrup,' said Friday.

'And if they're iron-deficient, they might not be thinking clearly,' added Melanie.

'Just stop it,' said the Headmaster. 'The last thing we need — in addition to three-quarters of the students wanting to vomit — is wild and reckless speculation. Everyone healthy is to return to their dorm rooms immediately and quarantine themselves until breakfast time. I'll call in a doctor, actually two or three doctors, to come and monitor the sick students during the night.'

Chapter 15

In the Room

Friday, Melanie and all the vegetarians were told to go back to their dorm rooms while the sick students were cared for.

'The whole thing is very odd,' said Melanie.

'The mass poisoning?' asked Friday.

'Yes,' said Melanie. 'It seems like such an enormous amount of effort. If you hate the school that much, why not just stay home?'

'Perhaps whoever did it has parents who won't let

them stay at home,' said Friday. 'Or their parents are overseas, so they have no home to go to.'

'Like you,' observed Melanie.

'I didn't do it,' said Friday.

'If you say so,' said Melanie.

'I didn't do it!' restated Friday.

'That's all right,' said Melanie. 'It doesn't bother me, either way. If you had poisoned the whole school, I'm sure you'd only do it for the best possible reasons. Underneath your ugly cardigan and eccentric green hat, you are an extremely good person.'

'I think I should say "thank you",' said Friday, 'because beneath all those insults was some sort of compliment.'

'That's what best friends are for,' said Melanie as she pushed open their dorm room door but then she stopped dead.

'Did you write that on the wall?' asked Melanie.

Friday followed Melanie into the room. On the wall the words 'Go Home Nerd' were scrawled in red.

'Of course I didn't,' said Friday.

'Then it must be directed at you,' said Melanie. 'If it was directed at me, it would say "Go Home Sleepy Head".'

Friday carefully stepped across the room to the words. She peered at the lettering.

'Is it written in blood?' asked Melanie.

Friday went white. She didn't like blood. She clapped her hands over her eyes. 'I hadn't thought of that,' she whimpered.

'I'll check,' said Melanie, following her over to the wall.

'How?' asked Friday. 'If it's blood, you mustn't touch it. We'll need to get expert forensic cleaners in to decontaminate the scene.'

'It's okay,' said Melanie. 'I'll just do what you always do.' Melanie leaned in and sniffed the lettering. 'Aha!'

'What is it?' asked Friday, peeking between her fingers.

Melanie dipped her finger in the letter then licked it.

'Urgh,' said Friday as she fainted.

'It's all right,' said Melanie. 'It's just strawberry syrup. The type you put on ice-cream.'

'It looks exactly like blood,' whimpered Friday from the floor.

'Who would do this?' asked Melanie.

'Someone who had just come from the kitchen,' said Friday. 'Perhaps it's someone who's angry that we thwarted their deathcap panic campaign?'

'Or perhaps it's someone with really strong feelings about immigration policy who thinks you should "go home" to Switzerland?' suggested Melanie.

'It's definitely someone trying to intimidate me,' said Friday.

'With strawberry topping,' added Melanie.

Friday gathered herself enough to stand up and go over to the wall. She dipped her finger in the lettering and tasted it herself. 'Mmm, tastes pretty good,' said Friday. 'Hey, I just realised we totally missed out on dinner.'

'I think that makes us the lucky ones,' said Melanie.

'If only we had some ice-cream to go with all this syrup,' said Friday.

'I've got a packet of biscuits Granny sent me,' said Melanie. 'They'd be pretty nice dipped in strawberry sauce.'

And so the girls got to eat some sort of make-shift dinner while they contemplated the strange goings-on of the evening.

Chapter 16

The Case of the Missing Furniture

Friday and Melanie were sitting on the lawn eating sandwiches. The whole school was eating lunch picnic-style because the dining hall was being scrubbed by professional cleaners to get the parmesan cheese smell out.

'Barnes!'

Friday flinched. Just what she needed. Someone else yelling at her. Friday turned to see Tristan Fanshaw striding towards her.

'Terrific,' said Friday. Her whole body slumped as she accepted that there was no way she could get away from him.

Tristan Fanshaw was a fifth form boy and nobody liked him. This was no exaggeration. Not even his own mother liked spending time with him. He was an entitled, mean-spirited, petty, pedantic snob, but the irritation he caused was beyond that. He didn't just insult and belittle others, he did so thoughtlessly. And the only thing worse than someone being maliciously cruel, is someone being thoughtlessly cruel.

'I need your help,' said Tristan. He beckoned for her to follow him.

'Really?' said Friday, not moving.

'I'm prepared to pay,' said Tristan.

'I can't imagine why I would help you otherwise,' said Friday.

'Yes, yes,' said Tristan dismissively. 'Come with me.' He started walking towards the senior boys' dormitory.

'Are you going to follow him?' asked Melanie.

'I suppose so,' said Friday. 'I've finished my sandwich and there's half an hour left of lunch to fill.'

She started ambling after him and Melanie followed in her wake.

'He walks quickly,' complained Melanie.

'He doesn't seem to have been affected by last night's mass poisoning,' observed Friday. 'He doesn't strike me as the vegetarian type.'

'He's poisonous enough already,' said Melanie. 'Ingesting extra poison probably wouldn't affect him.'

Friday had never been inside the senior boys' dormitory before. There was a lot of oak panelling and thick red carpet. It felt more like they were going to visit a high-price barrister in his chambers, than a seventeen-year-old in his school dorm room.

'This way,' said Tristan, clicking his fingers at them.

'He does realise we're not his staff, doesn't he?' asked Melanie.

'I think I am,' said Friday. 'If I take the case.'

When they caught up with Tristan he was unlocking his door.

'What's your problem?' asked Friday.

'It's easier just to show you,' said Tristan. He swung the door open.

Friday and Melanie stepped inside. Tristan was right. It was immediately apparent what his problem was – his furniture was missing. On one side of the room there was a bed, desk and chest of drawers typical of every Highcrest dorm room. On the other side of the room there was nothing except a scrunched-up set of sheets on the floor where the bed had been, books and stationery scattered on the floor by the window where the desk once stood, and a huge pile of clothes left in the chest of drawers' wake.

'As you can see, my furniture has disappeared,' said Tristan. 'My roommate still has a chest of drawers, bed and desk, but mine have vanished.'

'What happened?' asked Friday.

Tristan rolled his eyes. 'If I knew I wouldn't have had to hire you. I want you to sort this out and return my furniture to me A-S-A-P.'

'Asap?' asked Melanie.

'As soon as possible,' said Friday.

'Oh,' said Melanie. 'I hate it when people spell things.'

'When did it disappear?' asked Friday.

'Well, the bed was there last night when I slept in it,' said Tristan. 'The desk and chest of drawers, too. It was all here when I set off for breakfast, but when I came back here during mid-morning break to change my books, it was all gone.'

'So your furniture disappeared sometime between 7.30 and 11 am?' said Friday.

'That's what I just said,' said Tristan testily.

'Did anybody else in the dorm see anything?' asked Friday.

'I don't know,' said Tristan, 'I'm not going to waste my time playing detective. That's what I want you to do for me.'

'Do you have any enemies?' asked Friday.

'How should I know?' said Tristan. 'I can't read people's minds to know what they think of me.'

'I can answer that question,' said Melanie, holding up her hand. 'Yes, he does. In fact, it would be better to ask if he had any friends because that would be a much shorter list. Nobody likes him.'

'The feeling is mutual,' said Tristan. 'I don't like anybody here, either. Common riff-raff. If it weren't for the legal requirement to attend school, I'd be in Switzerland enjoying the first powder of the season.'

'You enjoy powder?' asked Friday. She knew rich people could be peculiar. But this was a peculiarity she had not encountered before.

'Powder snow,' said Melanie. 'He means he'd rather be skiing.'

'Snowboarding, actually,' corrected Tristan. 'Skiing is so twentieth century.'

'Is there anyone you have been particularly offensive to in the last twenty-four hours, aside from us?' asked Friday.

'I suppose I did tell Mr Maclean to his face that he was a disgrace to his profession, and that he had spinach stuck in his teeth,' said Tristan.

'He wouldn't like that,' said Melanie.

'I don't see why not,' said Tristan, with a shrug. 'It's much better to know than not to know. Besides, if he can't maintain proper dental hygiene he shouldn't eat spinach.'

'Anyone else?' asked Friday.

'My roommate, Harris, has gone off in a strop,' said Tristan. 'He's been sleeping on Singh and Thorpe's floor for the past week.'

'Then maybe that's why he took your furniture?' said Melanie.

'No,' said Friday. 'He could just take his own.'

'Why did Harris go off in a strop?' asked Melanie.

'I told him at the beginning of the year I'd chuck a glass of water on him if he snored,' said Tristan.

'And he snored?' asked Friday.

'Yes, he got an upper respiratory tract infection and snored like a chainsaw,' said Tristan. 'It was dashed inconvenient. I ended up throwing eight glasses of water on him in one night. I kept having to trot back and forth to the bathroom to fetch more. If I'd known, I would have borrowed a jug from the kitchen.'

'Surely making him wet would exacerbate his respiratory infection?' said Friday.

'Not my problem,' said Tristan. 'Getting some sleep was my main concern. He pushed off after two nights of it.'

'Anyone else?' asked Friday.

'I kicked a year seven boy into the swamp yesterday after breakfast,' said Tristan.

'Why?' asked Friday.

'He was crouching on the boardwalk, bending right over looking at a crab in the mud,' said Tristan. 'With his rear up in the air, he was practically inviting me to do it.'

'What was the boy's name?' asked Friday.

'I don't know,' said Tristan. 'He was a year seven.'

'They have names too,' said Melanie.

'Well, I don't bother learning them,' said Tristan.

'What did the boy look like?' asked Friday.

'Muddy,' said Tristan. 'I didn't see his face until he was trying to pull himself back up onto the boardwalk. He had landed head-first, so there was an inch-thick layer of mud over his whole face. He should have paid me for the privilege. Mud is supposed to be good for the skin, isn't it?' Tristan laughed at his own joke and wasn't at all perturbed when the girls did not join in.

'All right,' said Friday. 'I don't think we can get any more helpful information from talking to you. You can leave.'

'But this is my room,' said Tristan.

'If you want me to investigate, you need to leave,' said Friday. 'Because I'm not taking the case if I have to spend any more time in your company.'

'Fine,' said Tristan. 'I don't enjoy socialising with bluestockings, either.' He slouched out of the room.

'Why did he call us bluestockings?' asked Melanie.

'It's an eighteenth-century derogatory name for a female nerd,' said Friday.

'You've heard it before then?' asked Melanie.

'When you've been a nerd as long as I have, it

comes up from time to time,' said Friday.

'So what do we do now?' asked Melanie.

'We're going to experiment,' said Friday.

Chapter 17

The Secrets of the Furniture

'We need to figure out how the furniture was removed,' said Friday. 'The thief wouldn't have taken it through the door. There are eighteen bedrooms along this corridor, with thirty-six occupants. The chances of being discovered would be too high. They must have taken the furniture out through the window.'

Tristan's room had a large double window. Friday opened both panels wide. 'Look!' she said, pointing to the paintwork. There were large scrapes.

'Let's see how easy it would have been to do,' said Friday. She went over to Harris' bed and picked up the mattress, then promptly dropped it again. It flopped about and was hard to carry. Even with Melanie's help it took a lot of effort to get the mattress to the window then push it out.

'Phew, furniture theft is exhausting,' said Melanie.

'That was the easy bit,' said Friday. 'Now we've got to do the bed base.'

In the end it took Friday and Melanie fifteen minutes to shove all of Harris' furniture out the window. By which time they were knackered, Friday had a bruise in the middle of her forehead where she had been hit by the leg of the desk as it slid out the window and she had pulled several threads in her least ugly brown cardigan.

'Was that really worth doing?' asked Melanie as she looked out the window. The furniture looked sad sitting abandoned on the gravel road outside.

'Absolutely,' said Friday, swinging her leg over the frame and climbing outside herself. 'We've learned so much.'

'We have?' said Melanie, sitting on the frame and spinning her legs over before sliding herself carefully onto the drive.

'We've learned that our thief is physically strong and committed,' said Friday.

'Should be committed, more like,' said Melanie.

'That they are academically inclined and culturally refined,' said Friday.

'How do you deduce that?' asked Melanie.

'Because they stole a desk,' said Friday. 'Which means they intend to sit and work. Most students at this school don't actually use their desk as a desk. It's more of a collection point for their belongings. When they read or do their homework, they want to be as comfortable as possible so they sit on their bed. Our thief wanted a place they could sit and work diligently.'

'And how do you figure they are culturally refined?' asked Melanie.

'Because they stole the bed base,' said Friday. 'If all you're interested in is sleep, then you only need a mattress. If dignity and style is important to you, then you would value a bed base. It also tells us they intend to use the furniture for a while.'

'What does the chest of drawers tell you?' asked Melanie. 'Their mother's maiden name?'

'That they have nice clothes,' said Friday. 'If you have nice clothes, you care about how they are stored.'

'Is that why you always leave your ugly brown cardigan draped on the floor?' said Melanie.

Friday did not answer because she was too busy looking around her. She stood next to the chest of drawers doing a slow pirouette, taking in what she could see in every direction. To the north lay the long rolling lawn that stretched down to the edge of the swamp. To the west were the cricket pitches. Highcrest Academy had three. This was a fact the school liked to boast about in their prospectus. Although, in reality, very few students enjoyed playing cricket. Polo and lacrosse were more popular in their social milieu. Plus, in this day and age of helicopter parenting, sports involving extremely hard balls being purposefully bowled at great speed at an opponent's head were not as popular as they once were. To the south was the kitchen garden, then the formal flower garden that wrapped around to the front of the school.

Friday stood with her back to the dormitory, looking out at all this expanse.

'Can you see anything?' asked Melanie. 'Obviously you can, but I mean something more than the view of the empty school grounds that I can see?'

'I can see that the thief would have had to move

the furniture a long way,' said Friday, 'so they must have needed wheels.'

'A car?' suggested Melanie.

'Students aren't allowed to have cars,' said Friday. 'I think they used something simpler. Like a cart. Which they could have got from a place I can't see.'

'Now you're talking in riddles,' said Melanie.

'Mr Pilcher's shed is on the far side of the kitchen garden,' said Friday. 'I bet he has a cart. Let's go and visit him.'

Mr Pilcher was very hospitable when Friday asked if she could look around his shed. He made her and Melanie a cup of tea and gave them two of his own personal stash of cream biscuits before they got started. Friday was a favourite of his now. He was grateful for her faith in his mushroom selection. If he had been responsible for feeding deathcaps to 300 children, he never would have heard the end of it.

Mr Pilcher had two ride-on lawnmowers and even a small tractor, but he kept the key on him at all times. He didn't have a cart, but he did have a large wheelbarrow. Friday inspected it closely.

'Is your wheelbarrow always this spotlessly clean?' she asked.

'I like to take good care of all my equipment,' said Mr Pilcher.

'I can see that,' said Friday, looking about the shed. 'Everything is in excellent order. But a wheelbarrow would usually have traces of dirt or muck, whatever you had last carried in it. This wheelbarrow, however, is immaculate.'

Mr Pilcher came over for a close look. 'It is too,' he said.

'What did you last transport in it?' asked Friday.

'Um . . . well, it would have been the fertiliser for the rose beds,' said Mr Pilcher.

'What sort of fertiliser?' asked Friday.

'Horse muck,' said Mr Pilcher. 'The head groom is always very generous with the muck and it makes for excellent mulch.'

'Interesting,' said Friday. She leaned right into the basin of the wheelbarrow until her nose was barely millimetres from the bottom, then took a long, deep sniff.

'Gross,' said Melanie. 'Please just don't lick it.'

'It's all right,' said Friday, straightening up. 'In fact, it's quite pleasant. The wheelbarrow smells of lemons. It has been scrubbed with a soluble cleaning product. This is our thief's mode of transport. They would have cleaned the wheelbarrow so they wouldn't get horse muck on the mattress.'

'So the thief is a clean freak?' said Melanie.

'I don't think you have to be a clean freak to not want to sleep in horse muck,' said Friday. 'You just need a basic appreciation for cleanliness.'

'So that rules out 75 per cent of the boys at this school,' said Melanie.

'And it means we will soon catch the culprit,' said Friday, searching through her backpack before taking out a small jar and a large make-up brush, 'because there will be fingerprints on the handles.'

Friday started brushing dust over both black handles. Then she took out her magnifying glass and closely inspected the results. 'I don't believe it!'

'You recognise the fingerprints on sight?' asked Melanie.

'No, there are no fingerprints,' said Friday.

'The thief was a double amputee?' asked Melanie.

'No,' said Friday, 'they must have worn gloves.

Or wiped the handles clean. That's clever and thoughtful.'

'It sounds like someone who knows all about you,' said Melanie.

'Perhaps,' said Friday, as she took a moment to consider all the evidence. 'Who do we know who is strong, stylish, particular about clothes, clever, knows me well and is in need of a bed?'

'Can you make it a multiple choice question?' asked Melanie. 'You know I'm not good at linear thinking.'

'Is it a) Ian Wainscott, b) Ian Wainscott or c) Ian Wainscott?' said Friday.

'All of the above!' exclaimed Melanie.

'Exactly,' said Friday.

'But he's at another school that's hours away,' said Melanie.

'Do we know that for sure?' asked Friday. 'You know what his mother is like.'

'Obsessed with growing vegetables,' said Melanie.

'That would grow tedious quickly,' said Friday. 'He may have become fed up with living at home.'

'So where could he be?' asked Melanie.

'He would need a room,' said Friday. 'An empty

room. A place where he would know for sure that he wasn't going to be disturbed.'

'But there are students all over the school,' said Melanie. 'No room stays empty for long.'

'But there are lots of outbuildings and sheds around the grounds,' said Friday. 'I've got it!'

'You have?' said Melanie.

'You have brothers,' said Friday. 'You must know something about sport.'

'You've got two brothers, too,' said Melanie.

'Yes, but they're physicists, they don't count,' said Friday. 'Aren't some sports only played in certain seasons?'

'I believe so,' said Melanie.

'And its winter now,' said Friday. 'So which sports aren't played in winter?'

'Surfing,' said Melanie.

'At this school?' said Friday.

'Cricket,' said Melanie.

'That's right,' said Friday. 'It's only played in summer. So right now, in the middle of winter, the cricket dressing room would be entirely empty, and would stay that way for the next five months.'

It was a long walk to the cricket stand. Friday and Melanie had to cross two cricket pitches to get there. As they grew closer they could hear something.

'Is that music?' asked Melanie.

'He's not exactly being subtle about hiding his location, is he?' said Friday.

The girls walked around the back of the building. For modesty's sake, the window was eight feet off the ground so the players could have privacy while they were changing.

'I want to have a look,' said Friday. 'Can you give me a boost?'

'No,' said Melanie. 'Lifting other people up is not something I do.'

'Fair enough,' conceded Friday. She looked about. There was a metal garbage bin nearby. She picked it up and set it down by the wall, then carefully climbed up. When she stood on her tippy-toes she could just see in through the dirty window pane.

'What can you see?' asked Melanie.

'I can't believe it,' said Friday.

'Can't believe what?' asked Melanie.

'The way he's got it set up,' said Friday. 'It's just like . . . waaaaahhhh!'

Friday had stretched up on her toes too far, tipping the bin back. The bin toppled over and she fell forward, banging her head on the wall.

'Oww!' yelled Friday.

'Friday!' yelled Melanie.

'What's going on!' yelled Ian, as he burst out of the back door.

'Ian, it is you!' said Melanie. 'Friday is going to be so glad to see you when she regains consciousness.'

Friday was lying unconscious in a clump of large weeds. There was a large scrape across her forehead that was just starting to bleed.

'Urrrgh,' groaned Friday.

'What are you doing here?' demanded Ian.

'Tristan hired Friday to find his bed,' said Melanie.

'Typical,' said Ian. 'Trust her to fall in with the most amoral boy in school.'

'To be fair,' said Melanie, 'she didn't do it for moral reasons, she did it for the money.'

'Urrrrrgh,' moaned Friday.

'I suppose we should get her inside and stop the bleeding,' said Ian.

'How very thoughtful of you,' said Melanie.

Ian bent down and picked Friday up. She was not

heavy but she was a dead weight, so he staggered a bit as he stood up with her.

'I wish I had a camera,' said Melanie. 'This would be a great snapshot to be able to show your grandkids.'

'Would you mind getting the door?' asked Ian.

'Of course,' said Melanie.

Ian lumbered into the change room with Friday and dumped her on his bed. Well, to be strictly accurate, it was Tristan's bed. But Ian had gone a long way to make himself feel at home. The change rooms had been kitted out with all his personal belongings, including his doona from home. Even his school books were neatly stacked on his stolen desk.

'I like what you've done with the place,' said Melanie.

Ian went to the sink and wet a washcloth then walked over and dabbed it on Friday's bloody forehead.

'Oww!' wailed Friday, her eyes snapping open. 'What did you do to my head?'

'I'm administering first aid,' said Ian, dabbing her head a little more forcefully than he needed to.

'Oww!' said Friday. 'Stop it.'

'I wouldn't have to do this if you'd just left me well enough alone,' said Ian. He went over to the first-aid cupboard on the wall and took out a dressing and elasticated bandage.

'What are you even doing here?' asked Friday. 'You were expelled from Highcrest.'

'Thanks to you,' said Ian bitterly.

'I'm not the one who got the paper with the watermarks made up,' said Friday.

'But you were the goody-two-shoes who had to point it out to everyone, weren't you?' argued Ian.

'If you're so angry about everything I would have thought you'd be glad to get out of here,' said Friday.

Ian clammed up, pressing his lips together.

'Oh Friday, for a super-clever person you can be quite the dope sometimes,' said Melanie.

'What are you talking about?' said Friday.

'Ian is just like you,' said Melanie. 'He comes from a really dysfunctional family. This is his home.'

'Where does your mother think you are, anyway?' asked Friday. 'Won't she put out a missing person report when she realises you're missing?'

'She thinks I'm on a month-long hiking trip with an outward-bound group that specialises in helping young people come to terms with their anger issues,' said Ian.

'How did you convince her of that?' asked Friday.

'I got her to sign the application forms and drive me to the station,' said Ian. 'And I've arranged for someone who actually is on an outward-bound hiking trip to send her postcards from me once a week from remote locations.'

'You didn't pretend to poison the whole school last night, did you?' asked Friday.

'What?!' exclaimed Ian.

'Someone conducted an elaborate deathcap mushroom poisoning hoax,' explained Melanie.

'But it was stroganoff night!' exclaimed Ian. 'I can understand wanting to poison the school, but ruining such a good dinner, that's just wrong.'

'There have been a lot of strange things going on here since you left,' said Friday.

'We've missed having you around. You know what you should do?' said Melanie. 'Hire Friday to find out who framed you with the forged letters.'

'I'm not asking for favours,' said Ian.

'It wouldn't be a favour,' said Melanie. 'It would be like Tristan and the furniture. You'd be hiring her to do a job.'

'So I'd be the boss?' said Ian, smiling for the first time.

'Exactly,' said Melanie.

'Hey,' said Friday, 'I don't have to take the job.'

'Of course you do,' said Melanie. 'There is an irresistible mystery here. Someone fired all the teachers and framed Ian. Someone is stirring up trouble with the poisoning and the other weird things going on. You'd have to investigate that even if Ian wasn't your boyfriend.'

'He's not my boyfriend,' said Friday.

'No,' said Ian, 'now I'm your employer.'

'If I do take the job,' said Friday, 'what will you pay me?'

'I haven't got any money,' said Ian.

'I don't need money,' said Friday. 'My school fees are paid up for the next nine months.'

'What do you want?' asked Ian.

'I don't know,' said Friday. 'A favour. A blank cheque favour. I can ask you to do one thing at any time, no questions asked.'

'No way,' said Ian.

'Fine,' said Friday, starting to stand up, 'I'll get back to class.'

'All right, all right,' said Ian. 'You've got a deal. If you find out who framed me and get me re-admitted, I'll owe you one favour.'

They shook hands on it.

'What are we going to tell Tristan about his furniture?' asked Melanie, as she and Friday walked back to the main buildings of the school.

'We're going to return them,' said Friday.

'What?' exclaimed Melanie. 'But Ian's using them.'

'We'll just shove Harris' furniture across to Tristan's side of the room and tell him they're his,' said Friday.

'Isn't that immoral?' asked Melanie.

'Only if I accept payment for solving the case,' said Friday.

'Are you going to accept payment for solving the case?' asked Melanie.

'Of course,' said Friday. 'I'll give it to Harris. He deserves compensation for having to share a room with Tristan for so long.'

Chapter 18

▗▄▄▄▄▄▄▄▄▄▄▄▄▄▄▄▄▄

The Case of the Coloured Eyes

Friday wasn't sure how to start off in her investigation to clear Ian's name. She was sitting in study hall, tilting back in her chair and staring at the ceiling, which was usually something Melanie did, but in Friday's case she was wide awake and scowling with concentration.

'It's frustrating that we don't have internet access here,' said Friday. 'What I really need to do is investigate paper.'

'Paper?' said Melanie. 'What is there to know? It's flat. It's white. It absorbs ink.'

'I need to know more about watermarks, for a start,' said Friday. 'The stationery used to fire all the teachers was very elaborately forged. My general knowledge is much greater than the vast majority of the population, but even I have no idea how you would go about forging a watermark.'

'Ahem.'

Friday looked up. Gretel Dekker and Johanna Ottarson were politely standing over her. They were two tall blonde girls. Gretel was the school's badminton champion. Johanna looked like a surfer, but when she spoke she sounded like the Swedish chef from *The Muppet Show*.

'Can I help you?' asked Friday.

'I don't think Gretel really does have a scratchy throat,' said Melanie. 'So I'm pretty sure the only reason she would make that noise is because she wants your help but is too polite to disrupt you while you're thinking.'

'We do have a slight problem,' said Gretel. 'We don't know if it's something you could help with. But we don't know who to turn to.'

'A member of the teaching staff has more authority than me,' said Friday.

'But this situation was created by a member of the teaching staff,' said Johanna.

'It's VP Pete,' said Gretel. 'We're in his genealogy class. We tried complaining to him, but he just laughed and told us that independent problem-solving was part of the education process. We wouldn't learn if he solved our problems for us.'

'So what is the problem?' asked Friday.

'We're being bullied,' said Gretel.

'And he set this up?' said Melanie.

'Yes, to teach us about racism,' said Johanna.

'He's teaching you to be racist?' asked Melanie.

'No,' said Gretel.

'Actually, if you think about it, he kind of is,' said Johanna, looking confused as she came to the realisation herself.

'Okay, you'd better start from the beginning,' said Friday. 'What's going on?'

'Our class has been selected to take part in a sociological experiment,' explained Gretel.

'You poor things,' said Melanie. 'Getting selected for something is never good.'

'What's the experiment?' asked Friday.

'The blue eyes/brown eyes experiment,' said Johanna.

'Ah,' said Friday, 'the experiment developed the day after Martin Luther King Jr died to demonstrate for an all-white group of children how racism worked.'

'That's right,' said Gretel.

'How does it work?' asked Melanie. 'The experiment, I mean.'

'In the class all the children with brown eyes have to sit at the back of the room wearing brown collars, and the blue-eyed children sit at the front and are given preferential treatment,' explained Friday. 'Longer breaks, less work, extra courtesy, things like that.'

'That's right,' said Johanna. 'Except VP Pete is doing it the other way around. The brown-eyed children are getting preferential treatment.'

'And Mirabella Peterson is using it as an excuse to be really mean,' said Gretel.

'Mirabella is always mean,' said Melanie.

'But now she's getting away with it,' said Johanna. 'The worse she behaves, the more delighted

VP Pete is,' said Gretel. 'He says it shows that his experiment is really working.'

'And if anyone gets upset or cries about the bullying,' said Johanna, 'he's ecstatic. He says that shows we're really learning how terrible racism is.'

'I'll come and investigate,' said Friday.

'I'll come, too,' said Melanie.

'Thank you,' said Gretel. 'You've both got brown eyes, so you should be all right.'

'Although they were threatening to bring in a hazelnut test,' said Johanna.

'What's a hazelnut test?' asked Friday.

'They hold up a hazelnut next to your eye,' said Gretel. 'If your eye is darker than the hazelnut, you're considered superior to people with light brown eyes.'

'That's not in the original experimental method,' said Friday.

'No, Mirabella has been making improvements,' said Johanna. 'You'll see.'

Chapter 19

━━━━━━━━━━━━━━━━━━━━━━━

A Touch of Orwell

When the four girls arrived at the genealogy class they discovered that for the most part it looked like a regular classroom. The students' project work was pinned up on all the walls. And each student had researched a large and elaborate family tree, which had been illustrated with photos and portraits where possible. But at the front of the room there was a large banner saying:

BROWN EYES GOOD
BLUE EYES BAD

'I'm surprised,' said Friday.

'That VP Pete would allow this?' asked Gretel.

'That Mirabella managed to write a sign without making a spelling mistake,' said Friday.

'She didn't do it herself,' said Johanna. 'She made the blue-eyed students do it.'

Friday checked her watch. 'We've got five minutes until your class starts,' she said. 'I'll have a look around.'

The desks and chairs had been divided. Half the chairs were evenly spaced at the front of the room. The other half of the furniture was crammed into a corner at the back.

'Is that where the blue-eyed students have to sit?' asked Friday.

'That's where we sat last week,' said Gretel.

'This week, Mirabella decided we weren't good enough and we should sit on the floor,' said Johanna.

'Are you allowed to lie on the floor?' asked Melanie. 'You could just take a nap and forget about your worries.'

'We have to take notes for the brown-eyed students,' said Gretel.

'That's just cruel,' said Melanie.

Friday was studying one of the family trees on the wall. 'Look, here's Lizzie and Max Abercrombie's family.'

'They've got a lot of twins in their family tree,' observed Melanie. 'Even their dad has a twin. It's horrifying to think there's two of them.'

'Lizzie and Max won't speak of him in class,' said Gretel. 'They are ashamed of their uncle because he has a conviction for welfare fraud.'

'They're not ashamed that he's a criminal,' said Johanna. 'They're ashamed that he was on welfare.'

'It looks like they've got lots of interesting relatives,' said Friday. 'It says here that their grandmother was an aviatrix, their grandfather was a stationery magnate, their great grandfather was an advocate for domestic animal rights and their great great aunt won a bronze medal at the 1904 Olympics for croquet.'

'I didn't know croquet was an Olympic sport,' said Melanie.

'It isn't anymore,' said Friday. 'There were a lot of

silly sports included in the 1904 Olympics. Croquet, the plunge for distance, wax bullet duelling.'

'All sports are silly,' said Melanie. 'They just seem sillier because no one does them anymore.'

'This is intriguing,' said Friday. She had moved along to the next display.

'What is it?' asked Melanie.

'Mirabella Peterson's family tree,' said Friday.

Johanna rolled her eyes. 'Yes, we've heard about it endlessly. How her family has a long proud history in industrial cleaning products.'

'No,' said Friday, 'I mean this photograph of her parents. Have a look.'

The other three girls came over to have a closer see.

'Mirabella looks just like her parents,' said Melanie. 'The same chin, hair colour and forehead. It's uncanny.'

'Except her parents both have blue eyes,' said Friday.

'Oh, yes,' said Gretel.

'I'd never noticed that,' said Johanna.

'That probably explains why she has such an issue about it,' said Melanie. 'She might have felt like the odd one out at home.'

'What are you doing in here?'

The girls turned round to see Mirabella Peterson herself, standing in the doorway.

'Blue eyes are supposed to wait in the corridor until all the brown eyes are seated,' Mirabella reminded them.

Gretel and Johanna scurried out.

'And you two shouldn't be here at all,' said Mirabella. The rest of the class were filing in.

'I quite agree with that,' said VP Pete cheerfully, as he followed the students into the room. 'Are you two girls lost? Do I have to give you detention so you can spend some time studying your schedule more closely?'

'I thought you didn't believe in detention,' said Melanie.

'Flexibility is so important for an educator,' said VP Pete with a false smile. 'For you two, I'm prepared to make an exception.'

'We're here because you've been allowing Mirabella Peterson to unfairly persecute the blue-eyed students,' said Friday.

VP Pete chuckled. 'That's the whole point. I'm teaching my students empathy by demonstrating what injustice feels like.'

'That doesn't make any sense,' said Friday. 'That's like a geography teacher shoving his students out of an airplane to teach them what it feels like to be a raindrop.'

'Don't suggest that to Mr Maclean,' said Melanie. 'He just might do it.'

'Are you criticising my lesson plan?' asked VP Pete.

'Yes, I am,' said Friday. 'Any sane person would. But that is not the only reason why Mirabella's tyranny should be stopped immediately.'

'I wish you had blue eyes so I could shove you out in the corridor,' said Mirabella menacingly.

'I bet you do,' said Friday. 'But you can't, because my eyes are brown.'

'Not as brown as a hazelnut!' yelled Mirabella.

'No,' agreed Friday. 'But they're browner than yours.'

Everyone in the room gasped.

Melanie stepped closer to her best friend. 'Friday, I'm not sure if you've gone insane or if you're suffering from colour blindness but Mirabella's eyes are clearly as brown as a piece of dark chocolate.'

'No,' said Friday. 'That's not genetically possible.'

'Throw her out!' yelled Mirabella. 'She's an eye-colour traitor!'

'Look at the photo on her family tree,' said Friday. 'Both her parents have blue eyes. Blue eyes are a recessive gene. So it is genetically impossible for two blue-eyed people to have a brown-eyed child.'

Everyone gasped again and looked at Mirabella.

'So she's adopted?' asked Melanie.

'Of course not,' said Friday. 'She has every other genetic similarity. The pinched nose, the square jaw.'

'Then how are her eyes brown?' asked Gretel.

'Contact lenses,' said Friday.

'That's ridiculous,' said VP Pete.

'Physical vanity always is,' said Friday. 'But in teenage girls, it is a strong driving force. Thanks to increasing racial diversity in popular culture, blue eyes are no longer the cliché of beauty they once were. These days, the majority of music and movie stars have brown eyes. They are more fashionable. And Mirabella always wants to be fashionable.'

'Is this true?' asked VP Pete.

'You can't prove anything,' said Mirabella.

'I just have,' said Friday.

'She's right!' said Melanie, as she peered at

Mirabella. 'If you look really closely, you can see the edge of her contact lenses.'

'All right, all right!' said Mirabella. 'So I'm wearing brown-tinted contact lenses. That's not a crime. This dumb experiment wasn't my idea. No one said I had to have *naturally* brown eyes.'

'I'm disappointed in you,' said VP Pete. 'Cheating on a social experiment is very serious indeed.'

'No, actually, it's not,' said Friday. 'This experiment is the ridiculous thing. Students don't need lessons on how to be cruel to one another. They're all masters of it already. No one knows more about cruelty and intolerance than a teenage girl. The social pressure you've put on these students is just silly.' Friday turned to face the students. 'If you all refuse to participate, you will demonstrate your empathy far better than if you continue with this insulting charade.'

'I want to quit,' said Trea Babcock. 'Bullying is fine when it's off the cuff. But doing it every day is just boring.'

'Even I'm getting fed up with it,' admitted Mirabella. 'Coming up with new ways to make people miserable is not fun when it's homework.'

'We want Miss Darnston back,' said Gretel.

'Yeah,' agreed the rest of the class.

'So what do you say, Vice Principal?' asked Friday.

VP Pete was clearly fuming. 'You can each write a 5000-word analysis about what you've learned.'

The class groaned.

'You see,' said Friday. 'You've just demonstrated there are so many simpler ways to demonstrate what injustice feels like.'

Chapter 20

The Spinal Injury

Friday and Melanie spent the morning trying to break in to the Headmaster's office. This had not impressed the Headmaster because he was trying to have a nap at the time, and Friday's method of breaking-in involved drilling a hole through the stone external wall into the back of his filing cabinet.

'What on earth are you doing?' demanded the Headmaster as he leaned out his office window and found the two girls crouched in the bushes.

'We're attempting to work out who is behind the string of misdeeds that has taken place at Highcrest by reinvestigating the original crime,' said Friday.

'What?' asked the Headmaster.

'She's trying to figure out who forged the termination letters,' explained Melanie.

'We already know who did it!' said the Headmaster. 'It was Ian Wainscott.'

'Then how did he get the information?' asked Friday.

'I don't know,' said the Headmaster.

'Exactly,' said Friday. 'Which is why I'm trying to work out how someone could break in to your personnel files and find out all the teachers' dark secrets.'

'You just drilled a hole in the stone wall of a heritage-listed building!' yelled the Headmaster.

'Yes,' agreed Friday, 'and I've pulled Mr Braithwaite's file out of the back of your filing cabinet. So now we know it is possible.'

'Why didn't you just look and see if there was already another hole in the wall?' asked the Headmaster.

Friday looked about at the wall. There was only

one hole. The one she had just made. 'I suppose that would have been more sensible.'

'You promised me you would keep a low profile while the school was on probation,' said the Headmaster.

'I'm crouched in a bush,' said Friday. 'You can't get much more low profile than that.'

The Headmaster quivered with suppressed rage. 'I want to give you detention every day for the rest of your life, but the vice principal is at this very moment taking representatives of the Department of Education and the school council on a tour of the school, and I don't want to draw their attention to the fact that I have such a degenerate in the student body.'

'Thank you, sir,' said Melanie.

'Why are you thanking him?' asked Friday. 'He just called me a degenerate.'

'Yes, but the subtext is we're not getting detention,' said Melanie.

'Give me that file and get out of my sight!' said the Headmaster.

'If you stopped leaning out your window we would be out of your sight,' said Friday, as she handed the file to the Headmaster.

'And make sure you plug up that hole before you go. My office is draughty enough as it is,' said the Headmaster, slamming the window shut.

Friday and Melanie took a good twenty minutes to refill the hole with putty, then wandered as slowly as possible back to their classroom. They were supposed to be in woodwork but neither of them was in a hurry to get there. Unfortunately, as they turned the corner into the quadrangle, they came face to face with VP Pete and his tour group.

'Barnes,' said VP Pete. 'What are you doing out of class?'

'We were assisting the Headmaster with a problem,' said Friday.

'Something he couldn't cope with himself?' asked VP Pete. Two of the people in the tour group started jotting down notes.

'No, sir,' said Friday. 'The Headmaster is an excellent man, capable of anything.'

'Is this Friday Barnes?' asked a woman in the tour group. 'The student whose father was arrested for theft last term?'

'He was exonerated,' said Friday. 'He'd been framed.'

'That happens a lot here, doesn't it?' said VP Pete.

'My mother is a Nobel Laureate,' said Friday, trying to impress the group.

'Is she the woman who landed a helicopter on the polo pitch and caused four thousand dollars' worth of damage to the turf?' asked another member of the tour.

'She wasn't the one actually flying the helicopter,' said Friday. 'That was a member of the Swedish Air Force.'

More notes were jotted down.

VP Pete smiled. 'You'd better run along, Barnes. Thank you for being so informative.'

Friday and Melanie began to walk away.

'I don't think we helped,' said Melanie.

Suddenly they heard a crack, a sickening thud and then screaming.

'What was that?' asked Friday.

'It sounded like it came from the quadrangle,' said Melanie.

The girls rushed over to see. There was a large crowd gathered around a garden bed outside the English classrooms. Max Abercrombie was lying flat on his back in the middle of it. The balustrade along the verandah had collapsed and was lying in a scattering of sawdust on the ground.

'Urggh,' moaned Max.

His sister, Lizzie, was kneeling over him. 'Are you all right?' she asked, picking up his hand and giving it a squeeze.

'I don't know,' said Max. 'It's my back. It hurts so much. And I can't move my legs. I'm scared.'

'Gosh! It must be a spinal injury.' said Mr Conti, who was standing on the deck above them. The broken bannister hung splintered and dangling near his feet. 'Don't let him move! I'll run and call an ambulance.'

Mr Conti ran off.

'Should the only responsible adult be running away from the scene of a serious injury?' asked Melanie.

'He's probably gone into shock,' said Friday.

'Who, Max?' asked Melanie.

'No, Mr Conti,' said Friday. 'Teachers so rarely have to deal with anything important. He's not used to thinking like a rational adult.'

'Don't worry, Max,' said Lizzie. 'Help is on its way.'

VP Pete rushed over and pushed his way to the front of the crowd. 'What happened here?' he asked. His tour group hung at the back, observing the situation.

'Max was just leaning on the balustrade and it gave way,' said Lizzie.

VP Pete picked up a piece of broken timber that was lying on the ground. It had been a solid three-inch square piece of timber, but now it was splintered halfway through. 'Shoddy maintenance,' he said, shaking his head.

'What if I'm a paraplegic now?' asked Max.

'The school's insurance policy will pay for your rehabilitation,' said VP Pete.

'I'll never walk again,' moaned Max.

'You poor boy,' said VP Pete. 'This is a tragedy. A spinal injury could be the last straw for Highcrest.'

'He'll be fine,' said Friday. She was closely inspecting the broken balustrade in VP Pete's hand.

'What do you mean?' asked Lizzie. 'Just because you're a smartypants, doesn't mean you can diagnose spinal damage.'

'For all her brains, she doesn't know how to have an ounce of human compassion,' said Mirabella, who was at the front of the growing crowd of spectators.

'If you look at this balustrade,' said Friday, 'it's only splintered on one side, while the other half is a clean break.'

'So it snapped,' said Lizzie. 'They probably used substandard wood when they built it.'

'No, this is hard wood,' said Friday. 'You can tell because it's hard.' Friday tapped the piece of balustrade against the decking to demonstrate. 'And down here –' Friday kicked at the dirt beside Max '– we have sawdust. Broken wood does not make sawdust.'

'It was probably caused by termites,' said Lizzie. 'They weakened the wood.'

'Termites are photophobic,' said Friday. 'They only like the dark. They wouldn't eat a piece of wood that is exposed to daylight all day long. Besides, there is no papery disintegration of the timber like you would see if there was a termite infestation.'

'What are you saying?' asked Melanie.

'I'm saying that this balustrade was cut halfway through with a saw,' said Friday. 'The sawing action created the sawdust and the clean half of this break.

Then it would only have taken a good hard shove to snap through the rest.'

'It hardly matters,' said VP Pete. 'This boy is seriously hurt.'

'No, the only injuries Max has are very superficial,' said Friday.

'How can you say that?' demanded Lizzie. 'Can't you see my brother is in pain?'

'Yes, which is part of the problem,' said Friday. 'Also, I can see that his hand is reddened.'

'So he must have scraped it on something when he fell,' said Lizzie.

'Or he could have rubbed it raw when he was using a saw to cut the timber himself,' said Friday. 'If he did, he would have a blister on the inside of the base of his thumb. Show me your hand, Max.'

'Urrrgh,' said Max. 'I'm in too much pain.'

'That's another thing,' said Friday. She walked over and kicked Max's foot.

'Aaaagggh,' said Max.

'If you had a broken spine, you wouldn't be able to feel anything,' said Friday.

'But I can't move my legs,' said Max.

'That's probably a good thing,' said Friday. 'You

should stay as still as possible because I've just seen a spider crawl up your trouser leg.'

'What?!' exploded Max as he leapt to his feet and started dancing around, shaking his legs and madly patting at his trousers.

'What's going on? Is the boy all right?' asked the Headmaster as he and Mr Conti hurried to the scene.

'Everything is fine,' said Friday. 'Although you might want to bill the cost of repairing the balustrade to Max's family.'

'My father won't stand for this!' yelled Max.

'Let's write this off as hijinks,' said VP Pete. 'The balustrade will be easily repaired. It will give the year 10 woodwork class something useful to do.'

'Aren't you going to punish him?' asked Friday.

'We don't do punishments anymore,' said VP Pete. 'Max, I want you to write a self-analysis and have it on my desk first thing tomorrow. Everyone else get back to class now, or I'll be getting you all each to write a self-analysis too.'

The crowd scurried away.

'Come along,' said VP Pete to his tour group, 'I'll show you the dining hall.'

'Is that where the deathcap mushroom scare occurred?' asked a tour member as they walked away.

'That was odd,' said Melanie.

'What, that Max attempted insurance fraud?' asked Friday. 'It seems thoughtlessly spiteful and therefore in character.'

'Yes,' said Melanie, 'but to do something that involves a saw seems like such a lot of effort.'

'Some people aren't afraid of physical exertion,' said Friday.

Melanie shuddered. 'The fools.'

Chapter 21

The Cross Country

The next day Friday discovered that the Head-master had cooked up an even crueller way of punishing her than sending her to detention.

'I demand to see the Headmaster immediately!' said Friday. 'Please,' she added, realising it wasn't the receptionist's fault so there was no need to be rude.

'You have to make an appointment to see the Headmaster,' said Miss Priddock, the receptionist.

'Really?' said Friday. 'I never have before and I see him all the time.'

'That's because he's usually the one demanding to see you,' said Miss Priddock.

'The Headmaster had better see me immediately,' said Friday. 'Otherwise I might insist he needs an appointment to see me next time he wants some stolen property found or a mystery solved.'

'Barnes! Is that you I can hear yelling?' the Headmaster yelled from inside his office.

'Yes,' Friday yelled back.

'Get in here, then,' said the Headmaster. 'You're ruining my morning cup of tea, so you might as well come in and get whatever irritating demand you're going to make over with.'

Friday strode into the Headmaster's office. He was not behind his desk as usual but rather sitting in his armchair with his feet up on an ottoman as he sipped a cup of tea. And not from a mug, but from a proper teacup and saucer. He closed his eyes as he sipped and then sighed with appreciation.

'I didn't know you liked tea that much,' said Friday.

'I don't,' said the Headmaster, his eyes still closed.

'Dreadful dishwatery liquid. But my cardiologist says I need to drink less coffee and find ways to relax, and not let stress get to me.'

'Have the recent troubles here given you health problems?' asked Friday.

'My entire forty-year career has given me stress-related health problems,' said the Headmaster. 'But the last few months have certainly been the icing on the cake.'

'Why don't you retire?' asked Friday. 'No offence, but you are really old and you don't seem to find any pleasure in your work.'

'Gambling debts,' said the Headmaster.

'Ah,' said Friday. 'Still paying them off?'

The Headmaster nodded.

'You should try solving a bank robbery,' said Friday. 'It's a great way to earn a lot of cash quickly.'

'Some of us don't have your talent for busy-bodying,' said the Headmaster, opening his eyes and glaring at Friday. 'So, why are you here ruining my little tea ceremony?'

'Oh yes,' said Friday. 'I'm cross. When I returned to my room after breakfast this morning, I found this.' She reached into her pocket and pulled out a handful of paper torn into tiny scraps.

The Headmaster smiled. 'I enjoyed doing that.'

'It's my medical certificate,' said Friday. 'I got it from a real genuine doctor.'

'I'm sure you did,' said the Headmaster. 'It is nonetheless poppycock. There is no real medical reason why you should not participate in the school's cross country carnival.'

'The doctor said it would cause undue strain to my weak constitution,' said Friday.

'Balderdash,' said the Headmaster. 'You're perfectly capable of wading through the swamp, abseiling off the roof, or cutting your way through the school fence when you need to. By the way, the cost of repairs for that is going on your bill. A jog through the forest is entirely within the realm of your capabilities.'

'But . . .' said Friday, consternation overwhelming her ability to wrangle her vocabulary. 'But . . . I don't want to.'

'Ah, and that's the gist of it, isn't it?' said the Headmaster. 'Well, tough. You have to. Everyone has to. Students today spend too much time doing what they want and not enough time doing thoroughly unpleasant things just because they have to. That sort of thing used to be the backbone of the education system.'

'But the vice principal is supposed to be introducing new educational theories,' said Friday.

'My theory is that the vice principal is an idiot,' said the Headmaster. 'These progressive ideas are doing more harm than good. I'm taking a stand.'

'This isn't like you,' said Friday. 'Why are you choosing to put your foot down now?'

'Because this school is falling apart,' said the Headmaster.

'Has the school council been harassing you again?' asked Friday.

'Yes, but it's more than that,' said Headmaster. 'Highcrest is becoming a laughing stock. We need a PR coup. And that's what this cross country carnival is going to be. I've invited all the media outlets and they're turning out in force. They're all keen to get a look at elitist education. I intend to make their jaws drop at the quality of our grounds and facilities.'

'And making children jog,' said Friday.

'People love that sort of stuff,' said the Headmaster. 'It's schadenfreude. It makes them remember the days when they had to run cross country, and it fills them with warm gooey delight that they never have to do it ever again. Trust me, seeing three hundred kids running off into the forest, then eating a couple of dozen finger sandwiches before watching them come running back out again will make for a lovely afternoon.'

'But why do I have to participate?' said Friday.

'Everyone does,' said the Headmaster. 'There are no exceptions. Besides, with all your crime-solving, you're a minor local celebrity. Seeing you stagger out of the forest exhausted after a bracing five-kilometre run will emphasise my superb leadership of this school.'

'I won't do it,' said Friday.

'Then I'll expel you,' said the Headmaster.

'You wouldn't dare,' said Friday. 'You need me.'

'I have nothing left to lose,' said the Headmaster. 'If I don't pull this off, the trustees will use it as an excuse to sell the grounds off to a golf-course developer.'

'Not golf,' said Friday. 'Why is everyone so sports-obsessed?'

'I think rich people use it to distract them from their miserable lives,' said the Headmaster. 'Anyway, the long and the short of it is you're running. The whole course. No cheating or trickery. And you can tell Pelly no napping, either!'

'Okay,' agreed Friday, reluctantly. She didn't want to see the school shut down and the Headmaster lose his job.

Chapter 22

Actually Having to Run

'I can't believe we couldn't get out of this,' said Melanie.

'I know,' said Friday. 'If you combine my intelligence with your lethargy, we should have been able to find a way.'

'Have you got a race strategy?' asked Melanie.

'Run as far as the tree line,' said Friday. 'Then, as soon as we lose sight of the crowd, collapse in a heap and restrategise.'

'We could just take a shortcut through the trees and wait behind a bush until the other runners catch up, then rejoin the race?' suggested Melanie.

'No,' said Friday, 'that would be cheating. It wouldn't be fair on the people who are actually good at running. We'll just have to do the whole course. It should only take us an hour or two, at most. If we manage to not sprain our ankles.'

'Or get lost,' said Melanie.

'There are signposts throughout the course telling the runners where to go, so there's no danger of that,' said Friday.

'Runners, take your positions,' announced the Headmaster into a microphone.

'What does that mean?' asked Melanie.

'In our case, it means stand safely at the back so no one runs over the top of us,' said Friday.

'We are about to begin the Highcrest Academy's 69th annual cross country carnival,' said the Headmaster.

'I thought the school was seventy years old?' said Friday.

'They didn't run it in 1984,' said Melanie. 'The entire student body hid in the swamp and refused to come out until the event was cancelled.'

'I wish we'd thought of that,' said Friday.

The Headmaster raised his starter's pistol in the air.

'On your marks, get set . . .' yelled the Headmaster before he fired the pistol with a deafening CRACK.

Melanie instantly collapsed to the ground. Because they were at the back, none of the other runners noticed, they just took off running into the forest.

'She's been shot!' exclaimed Friday, falling to her knees beside her friend and taking her hand.

The Headmaster hurried over. 'What happened?' he demanded.

'She collapsed as soon as you fired the pistol,' said Friday. 'You didn't have real ammunition in there, did you?'

'Of course not,' said the Headmaster. 'It doesn't even take real ammunition. It's not that type of gun. There are no bullets, just a cap under the hammer.'

'She doesn't appear to have a gunshot wound,' said Friday, closely inspecting her friend before picking up her wrist. 'And her pulse is strong.'

Melanie snored softly.

'She's asleep!' exclaimed Friday.

'Typical,' said the Headmaster.

'Excuse me,' said a parent, pushing her way to the front of the crowd. 'I'm a doctor, well . . . a psychiatrist. Can I help?'

'If you want to have this child sectioned, I won't stand in your way,' said the Headmaster.

'She's just fallen asleep,' said Friday.

'I've seen this before,' said the psychiatrist. 'It's stress-induced narcolepsy.'

'What?' demanded the Headmaster.

'Narcolepsy,' said Friday. 'It's a psychological disorder where the sufferer copes with stress by shutting down and going to sleep.'

'How very convenient,' said the Headmaster.

'It's a tremendously difficult disorder to deal with,' said the psychiatrist.

'Don't worry, Melanie copes with it very well,' said Friday.

'We'd better get her to sick bay,' said the Headmaster.

'I'll come,' said Friday.

'No, you will not!' said the Headmaster. 'You've got a cross country to run.'

'But my best friend –' protested Friday.

'Will be perfectly fine without you,' said the Headmaster. 'Now run!'

Friday saw that the Headmaster meant business. He was clearly a man at the end of his tether. And spontaneous napping had never caused Melanie any harm before. So Friday turned to face the forest. She took a deep breath and started running.

Running is a deeply unpleasant sport at the best of times, but it is particularly awful when you're bad at it. There is so much unpleasantness at once. First, there is the shortness of breath, then the ache in the legs, then the sharp pain of the stitch, the soreness of the feet, the discomfort of the joints, and the lactic acid burn in the thighs. Eventually, some of this subsides with the increase of dizziness, delirium and sweating.

Then there are the added difficulties of cross-country running – scraping through prickly bushes, standing on sharp rocks, getting jabbed by sticks and wading through icy cold streams. Altogether, it was Friday's idea of hell. She had been running for a total of eleven minutes (an unprecedentedly long time for her) when the path she was running along came to a junction.

There was a bright orange arrow pointing left. Friday might have been brain-addled with exertion, but even she could follow this clear instruction. She lurched to her left and started running again before her legs seized up. And in this manner Friday continued along the course.

If she had been walking, she might have appreciated the impressive specimens of deciduous trees or local birdlife in the forest. But she needed all her concentration to desperately suck every breath into her lungs and stumble in the direction the arrows were pointing. Up ahead she could hear the footfalls of other runners, so she knew she was going the right way.

Friday had been running for nearly half an hour when she came up to another signpost. VP Pete was standing next to it, clapping for the passing runners.

'Well done, Barnes. Keep running,' said VP Pete.

Friday wasn't capable of speech so she grunted a response and veered off to the right, following the direction of the arrow. She knew she must be coming to the end of the course soon. Friday actually surged forward in an effort to run faster, just to get the whole ordeal over with sooner. Her legs were really burning now. She even had a shooting pain in her shoulder, which didn't make any sense because you don't use your shoulders to run. Friday closed her eyes and pushed on.

Suddenly she realised she had run into a bush. She must have stumbled off the path. Friday was well into the scrubby bush, so she kept moving forward to force her way out again. But as her foot plunged out the far side of the bush, the ground never seemed to come. Instead she was tumbling forward. Friday desperately tried to grab the bush and pull herself back, but as her weight dropped her grip wasn't tight enough and the branches slipped through her hands.

Friday fell.

Chapter 23

▰▰▰▰▰▰▰▰▰▰▰▰▰▰▰▰▰▰▰

Where Am I?

When Friday woke up she was aware of two things. One, she was cold. Two, everything hurt. Even her eyelids seemed to hurt, which was why she was reluctant to try opening them right away.

Friday's brain sluggishly tried to figure out what was going on. She had been running. It was awful. But why was she so cold? Why was it so windy? She would have to open her eyes to find out.

Friday gradually opened her eyes. She didn't

learn much straight away. All she could see was grey. Slowly, she realised it was clouds. She must be looking at the sky. Friday turned her head to see where she was. There was a big valley alongside her. Friday looked down.

'Aaaagggghhhh!'

Friday was not much of a screamer. She hadn't screamed when she was confronted by a swamp yeti, or when she was kidnapped by an escaped convict, or even when she thought she was going to have to attend a state high school. But she did scream now because she realised she was lying on a narrow ledge on the side of a cliff. There was a forty-metre drop below her, and a five-metre climb above her to the top. Friday moved so her back was hard against the cliff wall.

'Think, Friday, think,' she urged, talking to her own brain, trying to get it working.

Friday looked about. It was late in the afternoon. Probably about 4 o'clock. It was winter, so the sun would start to set in an hour. It was beginning to get cold already. It was only about eight or nine degrees, but it felt colder with the wind. And Friday was only wearing running shorts and a t-shirt. She pulled up her legs and hugged them to herself, trying to conserve warmth.

Friday looked over the side. She wasn't hallucinating. It was definitely a long drop. There was no way she could get down there. She twisted around and looked up. The top of the cliff seemed dauntingly far above her. And the cliff was sheer. There were no obvious toe or finger holds. Friday decided to stand up to get a closer look. As soon as she put her weight on her left leg, it buckled under her and she was overwhelmed by shooting pain. She nearly fell of the cliff again.

Friday closed her eyes tight and willed herself not to throw up. It was bad enough being stuck on a cliff in the cold when you're wet with sweat, without being covered in sick as well. Eventually the pain subsided to the level of a mere terrible throb. Friday opened her eyes and looked down at her leg. It was very swollen. There was an ugly purple discolouration of her skin emerging from her sock. As a scientist, Friday was curious to know what colour the rest of her foot was, but as a scared twelve-year-old girl she decided she would leave her shoe on. She was frightened enough already. Friday tried moving her foot.

There was the shooting pain again, so she sucked in her breath and counted backwards from one hundred while she waited for the pain to ease.

There was no way down and no way up, and if she stayed where she was it would be dark soon and she would very likely succumb to hypothermia. Friday looked about to see what resources she had. There was nothing except the rock face, which was warm now but which would soon drop to be colder than she was, sucking even more body heat from her.

But Friday was, if nothing else, logical. There was one remaining course of action open to her – yelling.

'HELP!' Friday cried. She paused and listened. She couldn't hear anything except the wind. 'HEEELLP!' she yelled again. She listened. Still nothing. Friday drew a deep breath. She had to keep trying. Being found in the next hour was her only hope. 'HEEEELLLLL . . .'

'Friday?' a voice called back. It was a long way away. But Friday could have sworn she heard her name.

'Gosh, I hope I'm not hallucinating from all the pain,' Friday said to herself. She sucked in a deep breath. 'HEEEEEEEELLLLLLP!!!'

'Friday!' the voice was closer now.

'Over here,' called Friday. 'I need help. I've hurt my ankle.'

Friday could hear someone running through the scrub above her. Her pain-addled brain processed this information much slower than it normally would.

'Don't worry, I'm coming!' cried Ian.

'Ian?' said Friday. His voice was too close. 'Ian, watch out for the cliff . . .'

'Waaahhh!' cried Ian.

Dirt and gravel fell on Friday's head. She looked up. Ian had fallen over the side and was dangling from the branch she had been dangling from half an hour earlier. His wrist strength must be better than hers.

'Can you climb back up?' asked Friday.

'I think so,' said Ian straining. His feet scrambled for traction as he pulled himself up, hand over hand.

'You're going to make it!' said Friday enthusiastically.

Suddenly the whole bush gave way. Ian's weight pulled it out of the ground by the roots, and he slid straight down the cliff face. Friday made an effort to catch him, but Ian weighed twice as much as she did, so he crashed down on her, squashing her into the ledge.

'Eurgh,' said Friday, gasping for breath. She felt like she had taken most of Ian's weight on her solar plexus.

'That didn't hurt as much as I expected falling off a cliff would,' said Ian. He scooted forward so his legs dangled over the ledge and he wasn't sitting on Friday anymore. 'Are you all right?'

'No,' Friday managed to weakly gasp between struggling for breath.

Ian looked at Friday. She was clearly in a lot of pain. And even in the last of the late afternoon light he could see that her lips were turning blue from cold.

'We need to warm you up,' said Ian. He pulled Friday up into a sitting position.

'Ow!' wailed Friday. Now her ribs hurt almost as much as her ankle. Suddenly something was being jammed over her head. Friday opened her eyes to find herself inside Ian's jumper. Her face was pressed against his neck as her head stuck out the head hole. 'Let me out, you're being ridiculous,' said Friday.

'*You're* being ridiculous,' said Ian. 'You're seriously injured. You're very cold and there is a good chance we are going to be stuck here all night. You need to warm up. You need to survive this so you can tell everyone how I heroically saved you.'

Friday wanted to argue but it was just too cosy and warm inside Ian's jumper. 'Mmm,' was all she managed. Ian wrapped his arm around her and pulled her closer.

'This is where you are lucky to be such a midget,' said Ian. 'If you were normal-sized you wouldn't fit in here, and there is no way I would take my jumper off for someone as annoying as you.'

'I don't understand how I managed to fall off a cliff,' mumbled Friday. 'I know I'm clumsy, but I followed the signs.'

'That was the problem,' said Ian. 'Someone re-arranged the signs so that they pointed in all different directions. Most of the school got lost. They muddled their way back eventually, but you were the only one who didn't turn up at all.'

'So you came looking for me?' said Friday.

'Of course,' said Ian. 'I'd hired you to find out who framed me. I couldn't let you off finishing the job.'

'Mmmm,' said Friday. She looked up at Ian. His eye was red and swollen.

'Has something happened to your eye?' asked Friday.

Ian laughed. 'It's just a bump.'

As the warmth from Ian seeped back into her body, she started to feel safe again, the adrenalin was easing away, and she began to drift to sleep.

'That's a good idea,' said Ian. 'You rest. I'm going to need you to give me a leg up so I can climb out of here in the morning, so you'll need your strength.'

Friday weakly snorted a laugh just as she drifted off.

Friday was lying in a field full of wildflowers. The sun was shining so brightly she had to keep her eyes closed. Someone was with her. Someone she liked. It was Ian. But she felt cold, very cold, and there was a loud noise that was getting louder. It was making a WHOP WHOP WHOP sound as the cold wind gusted stronger.

'Friday! Wake up!'

Friday wrenched her eyes open. She wasn't in a field. She was on a cliff ledge. It was night, but there was a bright light shining in her face. The noise and the gusty wind suddenly made sense. It was a rescue helicopter hovering above them.

Friday shielded her eyes to see what they were doing. A shape blocked out the spotlight for a moment. It was getting closer. Friday realised it was a paramedic being lowered down to the ledge they were on. The large man in a bright red jumpsuit and oversized helmet slowly descended towards them. The helicopter was buffeted by a gust of wind, and the paramedic slammed into the cliff face and fell the last metre onto the ledge, landing on Friday's sore leg.

'Oooww!' yelled Friday before losing consciousness again.

Chapter 24

▰▰▰▰▰▰▰▰▰▰▰▰▰▰▰▰

What Happened?

When Friday awoke she was in the sick bay. She looked across at the next bed. The paramedic in the red jumpsuit was lying there. He appeared to be in a great deal more pain than she was.

'You're awake,' said Melanie.

Friday turned the other way to see her best friend sitting in the chair alongside her.

'It makes a change for me to be the one awake and you to be taking a nap,' said Melanie.

'I didn't take a nap,' said Friday. 'I passed out from pain.'

'Ahuh,' said Melanie. 'I'll have to remember that excuse.'

'Is he all right?' asked Friday, indicating the paramedic.

'I should think so,' said Melanie. 'Dr Paviour gave him so much pain medication he won't know if he's Arthur or Martha. He's worse off than you. You've just got a severely sprained ankle. He's got a broken knee.'

'I feel partly to blame,' said Friday. 'If I hadn't been silly enough to fall off the cliff in the first place . . .'

'Don't blame yourself,' said Melanie. 'It's the person who altered the signs that caused the trouble. Besides, the paramedic would have been worse off if you hadn't been there to break his fall.'

'I seem to remember breaking Ian's fall as well,' said Friday.

'Oh yes,' said Melanie. 'He's completely unscathed. You'd never guess he'd spent four hours on a freezing cold ledge to look at him.'

'Is that how long we were out there?' asked Friday.

'It took a long time for the Headmaster to realise you were missing, not just running really slowly,' explained Melanie. 'Then he was naturally reluctant to call the emergency services while there was so much press around. Then Ian appeared, which was shocking in itself because technically he's expelled. Anyway, he yelled at the Headmaster that he was an incompetent old buffoon, in front of everyone. It was really very dramatic. Then Binky punched Ian . . .'

'Why?' asked Friday.

'He misses Debbie,' said Melanie. 'He still thinks Ian pulled the prank of firing all the teachers, which resulted in her getting airlifted back to Norway.'

'Poor Binky,' said Friday. 'We'll have to try to solve his problems next.'

'Then he took off running into the forest,' added Melanie

'Who? Binky?' asked Friday, rubbing her sore head.

'No, Ian,' said Melanie. 'He went off to look for you himself. He obviously found you.'

'I've got to see the Headmaster,' said Friday, throwing back her blanket and sitting up.

'But you're not well,' protested Melanie.

'Something serious is going on here,' said Friday. 'I've got to put a stop to it.'

'Are you sure?' asked Melanie. 'You could just be suffering concussion and the swelling in your brain is causing you to have delusions.'

'There's no time to waste,' said Friday, standing up. 'Oww!' Friday collapsed back on the bed. Her leg really hurt.

'There are some crutches in the closet, Would you like to try using those?' suggested Melanie.

'Why didn't you mention that earlier?' asked Friday as she gritted her teeth trying to suppress the pain.

'Well, everyone's always saying how super clever you are,' said Melanie. 'So it never occurred to me that you'd be stupid enough to try standing on that leg.'

Pretty soon Friday was hobbling towards the Headmaster's office with the aid of a pair of crutches. She was still in her cross country gear, but she was wearing a dressing gown from the sick bay over the top. Melanie came along too.

'What is the meaning of this?!' demanded the Headmaster as she barged into his office.

Friday hobbled over to the armchair and collapsed in it before looking around. She hadn't expected to find VP Pete, the Headmaster, Mr Abercrombie, Ian and an Asian man in golf knickerbockers crowded into the office drinking cups of tea. There was a tea tray set up on the Headmaster's desk.

'Am I interrupting something?' asked Friday, her head still fuzzy from pain and pain medication.

'Yes, you are!' yelled the Headmaster. 'Dr Paviour informs me that you are suffering from hypothermia and a sprained ankle. You should be in sick bay.'

'What are all these people doing here?' asked Friday.

'That is none of your business,' snapped VP Pete.

'I just had a near-death experience,' said Friday. 'Social niceties don't matter to me at the moment.'

'Did they ever?' asked Melanie.

'I know who you are,' said Friday indicating the Headmaster, VP Pete, Ian and Mr Abercrombie. 'But who is this? And why is he wearing such silly trousers?' She nodded towards the gentleman dressed for golf.

'How insufferably rude,' said Mr Abercrombie.

'This is Mr Musa,' said Ian. 'He's a businessman from Malaysia who is negotiating to buy the school to turn it into a golf resort. He flew in on his private plane to sign the papers.'

'You can't do that,' said Friday.

'Yes, I can. I have the full authority of the school council. I'm closing Highcrest Academy down,' said Mr Abercrombie. 'It is out of control. Highcrest has lurched from one disaster to the next. It is starting to endanger the lives of students.'

'Friday doesn't mind having her life endangered,' said Melanie. 'She does it all the time.'

'The trustees have decided to sell the buildings and grounds to Mr Musa,' said Mr Abercrombie.

'Can they do that?' Friday asked the Headmaster. 'It doesn't sound legal.'

'According to Sebastian Dowell's will, the school could be disbanded if ever the management of the school decides it to be dangerously undisciplined,' said the Headmaster.

'Which it has,' said Mr Abercrombie.

'But what happens to the money?' said Friday. 'Who gets that?'

'The Cat Protection Society,' said VP Pete. 'Apparently Mr Dowell liked kitties.'

'But selling the school would make millions,' said

Friday. 'What are they going to do? Feed the cats caviar and put them up in luxury penthouses?'

'The terms of Sebastian Dowell's will are none of your business,' said Mr Abercrombie.

'Yes, they are,' said Friday. 'Because this entire thing is a set-up. It's a conspiracy to push through this development deal.'

'She's delusional from pain,' said VP Pete, shaking his head sadly.

'I am not,' said Friday. 'And I can prove it.'

'If you can, please do,' said the Headmaster.

'Someone has been playing a series of nasty pranks, trying to cause chaos at the school and discredit the Headmaster,' said Friday.

'Poppycock!' said Mr Abercrombie. 'High-spirited students are just taking advantage of a leadership vacuum and total lack of discipline.'

'The poisoned stroganoff, the forged termination letters, the broken balustrade – they were all pranks to destabilise the Headmaster's position,' said Friday. 'The debacle of today's cross country was the final straw. If we find out who changed the signs around, we will know who has been committing all the pranks, and if we know who did it we'll soon be able to work out why.'

'How can we know who changed the signs?' asked Ian. 'The entire student body was in the forest at once. Anyone could have done it.'

'How many people got through the course and how many people got lost?' asked Friday.

'Of the 360 students at the school, 43 got through the course in good time,' said the Headmaster. 'The other 317 all got lost.'

'That's it, then,' said Friday. 'We know who did it.'

'When you say "we", you don't mean "me", do you?' said Melanie. 'Because I haven't been following what you've been saying at all.'

'The culprit is the person who came 43rd,' said Friday. 'Everyone who was ahead of them got through before the signs were changed. Everyone behind them got lost. So whoever it was must be the one who changed the signs.'

'That actually makes sense,' said the Headmaster. 'Does anyone know who came 43rd?'

'I do,' said Melanie. 'It was Lizzie Abercrombie.'

'How dare you!' said Mr Abercrombie.

VP Pete rolled his eyes. 'We can't possibly rely on the evidence of Melanie Pelly.'

'I remember quite clearly,' said Melanie. 'I woke

up as Lizzie and Max ran out of the forest. I remember the announcer saying that the brother and sister came 42nd and 43rd.'

'They ran out of the forest together?' asked Ian.

'Of course, they were in on it together,' said Friday. 'It fits. When the stroganoff was poisoned, Lizzie was the one to cast doubt on Mr Pilcher. And Max set up the balustrade fiasco. They must have been behind all the mishaps that have been happening.'

'This is outrageous,' said Mr Abercrombie. 'I'm calling my lawyer to begin proceedings for slander.' He took out his mobile and started dialling.

'Then there is the way in which you made your fortune, Mr Abercrombie,' said Friday. 'You're the son of a stationery magnate, aren't you?'

'Every time you say that I imagine a man being showered with money while he stands really still,' said Melanie.

'And what is stationery? It's paper,' said Friday. 'A man with a family background in paper would know how to get pink stationery printed up with a watermark featuring the face of his rival's son.'

'You did that? You set me up to take the blame, just because you don't like my dad?!' accused Ian. 'You ruined my life!'

'It explains why the forgery of your signature on the termination letters was so good,' said Friday. 'It *wasn't* forgery.'

'These are ridiculous allegations,' said Mr Abercrombie.

'Really?' said Friday. 'How much do you personally stand to gain from the deal to turn Highcrest into a golf resort?'

'I'm doing it for the good of the economy,' said Mr Abercrombie. 'It will create local jobs. And, of course, the cats get the lion's share of the money.'

'Ahem,' Mr Musa cleared his throat. 'He will have a ten per cent share. It's a standard fee for putting the deal together.'

'That's just compensation for my time and effort,' said Mr Abercrombie.

'I'm not good at maths, but even I know ten per cent of squillions is a lot,' said Melanie.

'Then there is the question of – why did you force the Headmaster to hire your brother to be vice principal?' asked Friday.

'What?!' demanded the Headmaster.

'His brother!' exclaimed Ian.

'If I'm not mistaken, VP Pete is Mr Abercrombie's identical twin brother,' said Friday.

'No way!' exclaimed Ian.

'I saw the Abercrombie family tree in the genea-logy classroom,' continued Friday. 'Twins run in their family. Mr Abercrombie has a brother who was convicted of committing welfare fraud. That sounds like a brother with nothing better to do than take a break from watching daytime TV to spend a few months impersonating a vice principal.'

'But Mr Abercrombie and VP Pete look nothing alike,' said Ian.

'No, but they would if VP Pete got a haircut, shaved his beard and lost thirty kilos,' said Friday. 'They are the same height and have the same hair colour.'

'These are outrageous accusations! No one will believe any of this!' said Mr Abercrombie.

'Plus, there is the lactose intolerance,' said Friday. 'Max and Lizzie are lactose-intolerant. They used that as their cover for not eating the beef stroganoff. And when I first met VP Pete, he told me that dairy did not agree with him, either.'

'I don't understand the relevance of this observa-tion,' said the Headmaster.

'Lactase deficiency, more commonly known as "lactose intolerance", is a heritable disease,' said

Friday. 'It runs in families. Max and Lizzie have it, and their uncle VP Pete has it as well. I wouldn't be surprised if Mr Abercrombie does, too.'

Friday lurched across the room to the Headmaster's desk and snatched up Mr Abercrombie's teacup. 'Let's see how you take your tea.' She looked into the cup. 'No milk.' She showed the cup to the room.

'You can't accuse a man on the basis that he drinks black tea!' snapped Mr Abercrombie.

'But it's the only explanation that makes complete sense of the facts,' said Friday. 'You hire your brother to destabilise the Headmaster, and you get your children to play dangerous pranks so you can make a percentage facilitating a major land deal.'

'I'm only making ten per cent,' protested Mr Abercrombie.

'It's the people at the Cat Protection Society who are going to make out like bandits,' said Melanie.

'And who is the treasurer of the Cat Protection Society? Who is going to take care of all that money?' asked Friday. She turned and looked meaningfully at Mr Abercrombie. 'That would be simple enough to discover. The Headmaster told me you were involved in several charities, and your grandfather was a pioneer in domestic animal rights.'

Mr Abercrombie stood quivering with rage for several moments before he launched into action. 'You've signed – that's final!' he snapped, as he grabbed up the paperwork and ran. VP Pete took off with him.

'Don't let them get away!' cried Friday. She started hobbling after them herself. Her ankle hurt dreadfully but thankfully it was so cold and the medication she had taken was so strong she was still able to give chase.

'I'll call the police,' said the Headmaster, as Friday clattered out of the admin building and began lumbering after the Abercrombie brothers running towards the swamp.

Chapter 25

The Chase

As she chased VP Pete and Mr Abercrombie across the school lawn, Friday could see where they were headed. At the end of the jetty, Mr Musa's private seaplane was tied up. Suddenly Ian raced past. He was chasing the men too and he was much faster on his feet than Friday.

Up ahead, Binky was standing on the jetty. He had been given the task of minding Mr Musa's plane. The Headmaster had been concerned that curious students might climb into the cockpit and start pressing buttons.

'Binky, tackle VP Pete!' bellowed the Headmaster.

Friday turned to see the Headmaster leaning out of his office window.

This would seem an odd request to most people. But Binky was not given to thinking about things. His headmaster had given him an instruction and he obeyed. As VP Pete and Mr Abercrombie ran down the hill towards him, Binky stepped forward and executed a superb rugby tackle on VP Pete, grabbing him around the waist and bringing him down hard on the bank of the swamp.

Mr Abercrombie kept running, showing a lack of concern for his brother that is sadly typical among many siblings.

Ian was swifter. By the time Mr Abercrombie ran onto the jetty, Ian was only twenty metres behind. Mr Abercrombie grabbed the rope that tied Mr Musa's water plane to the jetty, but Ian got to him just as he pulled open the door.

'You're not going anywhere,' said Ian, grabbing Mr Abercrombie by his jacket.

But, in a move of unexpected dexterity, Mr

Abercrombie slid out of his jacket, whipped it over Ian's head and pushed him into the water with an enormous splash.

'Ian!' cried Friday, who had made it to the jetty and was desperately limping to the spot where Ian was thrashing about in the water trying to right himself.

Friday threw herself down full length on the jetty, reached over the side and grabbed hold of Ian, pulling him to the surface. He took a big gasp of breath.

'Are you all right?' asked Friday, dragging Ian to the jetty so he could climb out.

Ian's response was drowned out by the sound of the plane's engine starting. Ian hauled himself up on the jetty and grabbed hold of the plane's door. He ripped it open and jumped in as the plane started to move.

'Wait for me!' cried Friday as she lunged in behind him. Her jump was nowhere near as athletic because her ankle still hurt, but she managed to get her upper body into the plane before it started speeding across the water. Ian grabbed hold of Friday and yanked her all the way in before it took to the air.

'Get out of the plane!' Mr Abercrombie turned and yelled at them.

'We can't, it's airborne!' yelled Ian.

'Great, now I'm going to be accused of kidnapping,' said Mr Abercrombie.

'And stealing a plane,' added Friday.

'Do you even know how to fly it?' asked Ian.

'Of course I do,' said Mr Abercrombie. Turning back to the controls, he put on the pilot's headset and started pushing buttons. Suddenly he cried, 'Ow!' and ripped the headset off.

'What's wrong?' asked Friday.

'There was a bee in the earpiece,' said Mr Abercrombie. 'I've been stung by a dead bee.'

'So you've got a sore ear, big deal,' said Ian.

'But I'm allergic!' said Mr Abercrombie. He looked genuinely terrified.

'How allergic?' asked Friday.

'Anaphylactic,' said Mr Abercrombie.

'Is that bad?' asked Ian.

'See for yourself,' said Friday.

Mr Abercrombie's face was starting to turn red before their eyes. He was clutching at his throat, rasping for breath.

'Stop grabbing your throat and fly the plane!' yelled Ian.

Mr Abercrombie didn't respond. He was too busy trying to drag oxygen into his lungs through his tightening throat.

'He needs an emergency tracheotomy right now or he is going to die,' said Friday. 'You're going to have to fly the plane.'

'Me?!' cried Ian.

'There's no one else,' said Friday as she reached forward, grabbed Mr Abercrombie by the shoulders and pulled him backwards out of the pilot seat. 'Relax, Mr Abercrombie, 94 per cent of patients survive this procedure . . . although most of them have it performed by a qualified doctor, which would help.'

'Do you have any tips on how to do this?' asked Ian as he climbed over and took the controls.

'You've played computer games, haven't you?' said Friday. 'I'm sure it's much the same principle – up is up, down is down, fuel is good, no fuel is bad. The only difference is, unlike a computer game, if you screw it up you don't get a second and third life.'

'Thanks for the pep talk,' said Ian.

Friday returned her attention to her patient. 'I don't suppose you have a pen and a really sharp knife?

I normally would, but I don't carry those things in my running clothes.'

Mr Abercrombie was going purple from lack of oxygen but he still waved his hands at Friday desperately trying to dissuade her from performing surgery.

'Ah! That's perfect,' said Friday, spotting the plane's first-aid kit strapped to the wall. She opened it up. 'It's got everything we need. Even antiseptic, which is good for you.' She poured antiseptic over the base of Mr Abercrombie's throat.

'Gargggh!' Mr Abercrombie used the last of his breath to emit a strangled scream before passing out.

Friday picked up the scalpel and reached down to Mr Abercrombie's thorax. Suddenly the plane lurched to one side and Friday fell across Mr Abercrombie's chest.

'What was that?' she demanded.

'I had to swerve to miss a bat,' said Ian.

'Can't you keep this plane still while I'm cutting open this man's throat?' said Friday.

'Excuse me if my attempt at flying a plane for the first time doesn't meet your high standards,' said Ian.

Friday pulled herself upright, deftly slit a hole in Mr Abercrombie's skin and pushed a small tube down into his throat, allowing air to pass into his lungs. She could hear the hiss of his breath going in and out.

'It worked!' cried Friday delightedly. 'I've read about the procedure so many times in books, but it's still fun when it actually works in real life. Thankfully, there's surprisingly little blood.'

'I'm thrilled for you,' said Ian sarcastically. 'Now you've saved his life, we can all die together when I crash this plane.'

Friday climbed forward into the co-pilot's seat next to Ian. 'What's with all the negative self-talk?' she asked. 'It's not like you.'

'That's because I'm not normally in life and death situations where I have no idea what to do,' said Ian as he raised the flaps and pulled back on the throttle.

'What are you doing now, then?' asked Friday.

'Adjusting our angle of descent and reducing speed,' said Ian. 'I thought that would be a good start.'

'Less speed certainly sounds like a good idea,' said Friday. 'And you're going to land it on the water, which is a good thing because it's much softer than land.'

'Water filled with sharks,' said Ian. He was skimming along just above the water now.

'I don't want to alarm you but the bank of the swamp seems to be rapidly approaching,' said Friday. Looking out ahead of them, she could see the lights from the school and several lights on the jetty, where no doubt people were gathered watching them.

Ian swore. He'd been so busy concentrating on the dials and the plane's altitude above the water he had forgotten to look out for land. He panicked and pulled back the throttle so that the engines stalled completely. The plane dropped hard onto the water, but still had enough forward momentum that they skipped forward across it like a huge stone.

'We're going to hit!' cried Friday.

'There's nothing I can do,' said Ian. 'This thing doesn't have a brake pedal.'

'Brace yourself,' said Friday. She wrapped herself in the foetal position then felt Ian's arms wrap around her, before there was a crunch. But it was a surprisingly small crunch.

They both looked up to see that the plane's nose had hit the bank but not very hard. The only visible damaged was one bent propeller.

'I can't believe I landed a plane,' said Ian.

Chapter 26

▰▰▰▰▰▰▰▰▰▰▰▰▰▰▰▰

Resolution

It took several hours for everything to get sorted out. The paramedic from sick bay had hobbled down to the swamp to monitor Mr Abercrombie's condition until an ambulance arrived. But Sergeant Crowley got there first, so Mr Abercrombie was handcuffed to the gurney before he was rolled into the back of the ambulance.

VP Pete was arrested as well, much to the delight of the student body and teaching staff. Word soon got around. As he was led in handcuffs to the police squad car, the entire school lined the driveway, dressed in their pyjamas and dressing gowns, so they could cheer and clap as he was taken away.

The Headmaster held an impromptu school assembly on the front steps of the school at 3 am.

'Students, teachers, I am pleased to announce that this ordeal in progressive education is now over,' said the Headmaster.

Everyone cheered.

'The school council has been so embarrassed by forcing me to hire a man with a criminal record to act as vice principal that they have no credibility if they try to interfere in school matters again,' said the Headmaster. 'And the school council won't be sticking its nose in anymore, because it will take them months to elect a new president.'

There was more applause.

'I'd like to take this opportunity to publicly apologise to Ian Wainscott,' said the Headmaster. 'He will be reinstated with full scholarship immediately.'

Everyone cheered again.

'Hey, wait,' said Mirabella. 'Ian's the scholarship kid? I thought it was Friday.'

'Shut up, Mirabella,' said Melanie.

'To celebrate this wonderful occasion I have asked Mrs Marigold to open up the kitchen,' said the Headmaster. 'Everyone will be served with as much ice-cream as they can eat!'

The cheering was louder than ever as the whole school joyfully wandered off towards the dining hall.

Friday was looking a bit miffed.

'Something wrong, Friday?' asked the Headmaster.

'I notice you apologised to Ian, but no words of thanks for me,' said Friday.

The Headmaster laughed. 'I can't let people know the extent of your role as an intellectual enforcer at this school.'

'Why not?' asked Friday. 'Don't you think I deserve some credit? I did just save the school and perform an emergency tracheotomy in a moving airplane.'

'Because if people found out, I'd be locked up either in a prison cell or a lunatic asylum,' said the Headmaster. 'And after forty years in education, I'd prefer not to get locked up in another institution.'

Friday pouted, and kicked at the gravel driveway.

Then wished she hadn't because her ankle still hurt.

'Come on, Barnes,' said the Headmaster. 'You've got your free tuition and you solved the case. You don't really want fame and glory as well. People would expect you to wear smarter clothes.'

'True,' agreed Friday begrudgingly.

'Let's go and eat ice-cream,' said the Headmaster. 'I have my own stash of chocolate sprinkles, and as a personal mark of my gratitude I'm prepared to share them with you.'

As the sun rose over Highcrest Academy the entire student body was enjoying their second, and in some cases, third or fourth, helpings of ice-cream. The Headmaster had even decreed that everyone could go back to bed and sleep in for the first two periods of the day, which had made Melanie leap up and kiss him on the cheek. It seemed like the perfect start to a new day on the heels of a very long one.

Ian slid into the seat next to Friday.

'I suppose thanks are in order,' said Ian. 'You cleared my name.'

Friday smiled. 'You don't have to thank me. You were my client. I did it for payment.'

'What do you mean?' asked Ian.

'The deal was that I cleared your name and then you owed me a favour,' said Friday. 'That's thanks enough. I'm going to enjoy having that favour up my sleeve.'

'Hang on,' said Ian. 'I saved your life. I found you on the cliff face.'

'You fell on me,' said Friday.

'Then shared my jumper with you,' said Ian.

'You did?' said Melanie. 'How romantic. You didn't tell me that, Friday.'

'You didn't bring a mobile phone or any way of attracting the attention of rescuers,' said Friday.

'She's very particular about acts of heroism, isn't she?' Ian said to Melanie.

'She's just feeling vulnerable because you didn't just rescue her physically but emotionally as well,' said Melanie.

'I am not!' said Friday.

'See how red her face is getting?' said Melanie. 'She's embarrassed because I'm speaking the truth.'

Friday stared at her bowl of ice-cream and tried to will her face back to normal colour.

'Oh no!' exclaimed Ian. 'What's going on?!'

Friday looked up to see what had shocked Ian. It was a man she recognised.

'Mr Wainscott?!' exclaimed Friday. 'What are you doing here?'

The last time Friday had seen Ian's father he'd been yelling abuse at her as he was dragged away by police because she had just proven that he was guilty of bank robbery and insurance fraud.

'I've come to claim custody of my son,' said Mr Wainscott.

To be continued . . .

To find out what happens next, read the
fifth book in the series . . .

FRIDAY BARNES
The Plot Thickens

Publishing in 2016

To find out what happens next read the fifth book in the series . . .

R. A. Spratt

FRIDAY BARNES
Girl Detective

R. A. Spratt

FRIDAY BARNES
Under Suspicion

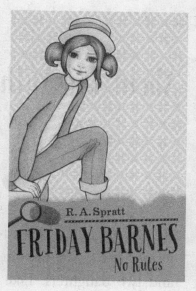

COLLECT THEM ALL!

About the Author

R. A. Spratt is an award-winning author and television writer. She lives in Bowral with her husband and two daughters. Like Friday Barnes, she enjoys wearing a silly hat.

For more information, visit www.raspratt.com